Maya Loop

Lis Anna-Langston

[signature]

~ Mapleton Press ~

Other Novels by Lis Anna-Langston

Gobbledy

Tupelo Honey

Skinny Dipping in a Dirty Pond

Tolstoy & the Checkout Girl

Maya Loop
Lis Anna-Langston
www.lisannalangston.com
©2021 Lis Anna-Langston – All Rights Reserved
Cover & Interior Art by Anastasia Khmelevska

Mapleton Press
First Edition
South Carolina
ISBN: 978-1-0879-4306-0
Printed in the United States of America
Library of Congress Catalog Number: 2020925821

For Mark…

Who *leaps* with me.

In the beginning …

Lightning cracks across the sky. Charged particles burn through the atmosphere. I watch from the kitchen window. White and blue speckles light up the cracked bistro table in a brilliant flash. My eyes settle on the refrigerator. Black eyes twist like storms and stare back at me from a drawing. Rain pounds against the window. A flickering ball of light appears out in the hallway. It sweeps over the dark ceiling like a strange code, darting in and out of the kitchen. Pre-dawn sits in shadows. The light descends the creaky staircase in the main hallway. I pull on my glitter green combat boots and follow.

Under the torn awning of my apartment building, I stop, looking for the light. A scratching gets my attention. Looking for clues, I find a sparrow huddled against the bricks. My plastic raincoat crinkles as I kneel down to inspect. The bird's wings are too wet to fly. Raising the sparrow to my cheek, its tiny heartbeat pulses against my skin. Without warning it jumps from palm to shoulder, using the storm wind to carry it along. Rustling under my plastic raincoat, it perches comfortably in the curve of my neck.

I pull a flashlight from my pocket, smack it against my palm to jostle the batteries, and flip the switch. A dim trail of light cuts a path and I enter the storm with the sparrow.

At the end of the block I stop at the intersection and wait for the light to change. Deep in my gut a feeling arises. There is a right way and a wrong way to turn. This has never occurred to me while running down the sidewalks of Baltimore. There are no cars, no people. Just me and a storm and a sparrow. Just me and one chance to turn in the right direction.

Wind and water whip around my face as I ask, "Do you know who I am?"

"You are Maya Loop," the sparrow says.

Confused, I look up and down the empty streets. "How do you know my name?"

"You don't have much time left," the sparrow says.

"For what?"

The sparrow walks to the end of my shoulder, holding tight. A fierce wind whips down the street making the streetlights sway. Lightning flares across the blank canvas of night. I turn to face him and for the first time realize he's blind.

His milky white eyes focus on nothing but his voice is firm. "Hold out your hands."

Stuffing the flashlight into my pocket it continues to glow as I hold my hands out. My palms quickly fill with rainwater, creating tiny puddles. An image takes shape in the reflection, like a strange fortune teller's ball. An image of black-eyed monsters.

"They're coming," the blind sparrow says.

Chapter One

Waking from the dream I pull my favorite cheetah blanket tight and swallow back the dry taste in my mouth. A hollow feeling of goodbye fills the room. Holding my blanket tight, I stare at the tiny pieces of yellowed tape stuck to the wall. All of my wonderful drawings of fantastical bugs have been taken down, rolled, and shoved in a cardboard tube. I don't have to see the rest of the room to know my whole world is falling apart. Just the tape. Remnants. Reminders. Pieces. That's all that's left. Pieces of ripped tape. This has been my bedroom for ten years. Now it's almost empty. One sleeping bag. One pillow. One cheetah blanket. Check.

And it's raining.

Because nothing says goodbye like rain.

Car horns honk below. The room is gray and dim.

The smell of spicy takeout from Fong's Kitchen drifts down the street. Everything I know is about to change and I lay quietly wishing it all away. Away with it all, I think, squeezing my fists tight. If I wish it all away repeatedly then I can turn back time and make this moment never happen. And I want that more than anything. To make this moment never happen.

Baltimore is my favorite place in all the world but it hasn't been easy lately. People complain about the curfew. It doesn't bother me so much. Too much hides in darkness. I'm perfectly content to sit at the small kitchen table and chat with my friend Totsie. The one who put purple finger paint on my nose, traded a grape juice box for a pink lemonade back when I was three years old. A friendship was born. That was eight years ago. A lifetime ago. Almost a decade. *#Sigh.*

Rain picks up and I roll over, staring out the window. An old window. The kind with panes. Raindrops hit the glass and roll into puddles on the small strip of grass seven floors below. It isn't really grass. Planted on the north side of the building it never gets sunlight. It stays brown year-round. It's funny how much I miss that brown grass now that I know I can't have it anymore. The crunchy prickle under my bare feet. How early morning frost clings to its weathered tips when I walk to school in autumn.

Pigeons huddle on the wires outside my window dodging rain. I like birds and bugs and imagine the coos and calls are answers to questions I haven't asked yet. Beyond those birds, the best second-hand store in the entire world is three blocks away. The one where I found my glitter green combat boots, scuffed on the toes, laying sideways on the hardwood floor next to my suitcase.

There was a book my parents read to me when I was little where you said goodnight to all of the things in a room and then goodnight to the moon. A brick building across the narrow street blocks out my view of the sky but remembering the book makes me want to say goodbye to everything in my room.

Goodbye chipped baseboard we never found the time to paint.

Goodbye old windowpanes that frame the pigeons.

Goodbye best bedroom in the world.

Goodbye cold hardwood floor made bearable by magical unicorn slippers.

Goodbye pieces of tape that held my wild and wonderful drawings in place.

I press my face into my pillow and whisper desperately, "Goodbye, old life. This sucks."

Total drama llama statement. Totsie has a saying, "Sometimes when everything feels like it's falling apart, it's really falling together."

Please, let that be true.

I'm trying not to be mad. My mom wants us to have more than a tiny apartment. With only one bedroom, she sleeps on the couch. Maybe she's right. Maybe it isn't how to live but it's been our way for so long. We were going to move out of the apartment when my dad started losing his balance. After he fell down the front steps of the building, running to grab my stuffed duck named Mr. Wibbles, the neighbors called an ambulance. The night he came home from the hospital he drew a cartoon on my wall of me and Wibbles. A crazy cartoon where me and Wibbles save the world. The next five months he stayed in bed and was dead before summer.

He left me two things. An old digital camera and his sketchbook. I've never opened the sketchbook. Not once. It was his whole life and opening it feels like admitting he has no life anymore. The camera is different. I created a video of the wall but don't understand how I'm ever supposed to leave that piece of my life behind. My dad was the best cartoonist in the world. Now the superintendent will paint over my life and make it disappear. It makes me so mad. Maybe I'll rewind time all the way back before that day. To that day when Mr. Wibbles fell to the bottom of the concrete steps. Rewind back to that day in a wild loop of time. That's all time is. Day after day tumbling forward endlessly.

Loop.

Like me.

And my parents. They're both named Charlie. What are the odds, really? Granddaddy tells a story about how doctors said my mom was a boy and he got so set on that name he couldn't change. He's like that. Getting set on things and not wanting to change.

A tiny ladybug lands on the other side of the window. Laying my finger on the glass, I pretend we're touching. Everyone at school squashes bugs except Totsie.

Forcing myself out of bed I stand in the middle of my bedroom and whisper, "I love you, Charlie Loop," covering all bases, past, and present. The words stick deep in the walls I'm leaving forever. Over and over I repeat the words, squeezing my fists tight. Deep in the walls, the words go. Deep into the walls my hopes and wishes go to hide. Deep in the walls, all of my secrets wait until one day the words echo back like I never left at all.

Chapter Two

The rental car is cramped and smells like plastic. I can feel my mom staring.

"We'll see each other again before you know it," my mother says. A statement injected with too much cheer to be convincing.

"How can you be so happy about everything falling apart?"

Gold light shimmers over the treetops. Magic colors mixed with dread. Fresh grass and purple-tipped flowers line the roadside, a reminder that every petal takes me farther from home. I glance back out the window. Storm clouds are behind us now. We left the rain in Baltimore.

My mom steers the rental car off the small, two-lane highway into the parking lot of a gas station. Faded signs hang in the window advertising products I've never even heard of before. Beechwood gum. RC Cola. A bell dings when a car stops at the pump. This place is Hickville for sure.

In a very serious tone my mother says, "I don't mean to scare you," then stops long enough to throw the car into park, "but being a cop in Baltimore isn't getting us anywhere. Do you understand that my partner was killed in the line of duty right in front of me? There are things I try to shield you from but I refuse to lie to you. The danger pay on this new job alone is five times what I'd make in Baltimore on the beat. Look, I know you don't understand salaries and compound interest but I must make this leap for us and you will have to leap, too."

Loops making leaps.

What's a girl to do?

Gray sky rolls across the open field across from the gas station. All that space is overwhelming. I feel so numb it's like my brain is going to ooze from my ears. In my mind, I conjure buildings, brick by brick. The grocer on the corner. The man who lives one block over with three TVs mounted to his wall that play 24/7. The broken windows on the way to Totsie's apartment, the middle school seven blocks from my front door, Fong's Kitchen, Dressed Up Consignment.

A city full of people.

Gone.

For danger pay.

Whatever that is.

"Maya?" my mom whispers.

The gentle hum of the car engine is hypnotic. The last car we owned was my dad's powder blue Impala. After it was stolen, my mother replaced it with the city bus. I sigh. Baltimore was hard. I just don't understand how leaving is supposed to be easy.

"Yes?"

"Can you do this? For me? For us?"

"Us" is a sensitive subject. Especially since "us" gets smaller and smaller. I am about to answer when a sharp, unexpected breath fills my lungs. Clean, country air hovers in the car. Mr. Wibbles stares up from my lap. Totsie and my mom are the only ones who know about Mr. Wibbles. I love Wibbles. I don't care if he's a baby toy. I look down at his funny little duck body squeezed into a fox costume.

"What if something happens to you?"

Charlie Loop laughs. "Girl, I survived eight years on the B-more PD. Have a little faith in the Loops. Besides, my new role as a contractor provides me with round the clock security. It's you I'm worried about," she says, reaching over to tickle my ribcage. "You're gonna be out there in the country with all those crazy bugs and UFO sightings and daddy with all his pickle making skills. He just might pickle you. You're gonna have to live off canned biscuits because he never learned to cook."

My mom pushes her index finger into my ribs. Wibbles tumbles to the floorboard in the ticklefest. Reaching forward, I giggle. At first, it's low and nervous but pretty soon the rental car is full of squealing, twisting, turning laughter. Laughter that makes my bones feel hollow and light, a great trembling that shakes the tips of my blue hair and clears the heavy heart I've propped up for days. I suck in a deep breath and hold it but instead of exhaling, my roaring laughter turns to tears. At first, it feels like I'm still laughing. Tears are tricky like that.

My mother pulls away. "Maya—are you okay?"

"Yes—I don't know. I'm sorry." Crying laughter. It's all the rage.

"Oh, my sweet girl," my mom whispers, twisting awkwardly in the driver's seat for a hug. "We're okay. We're going to be okay."

"You don't know that."

Squeezing me tight she whispers, "I do know that. You are the bravest little girl I have ever met."

That makes me cry harder. I am not the bravest little girl in the world. I am terrified of the dark and that awful scratching sound in the walls during winter. But I don't want to talk about all the things that scare me so I blurt out, "What am I going to do without the internet?"

Charlie Loop laughs again. "Is that what all this drama is about? Plenty of people got along just fine without the internet. Trust me."

#Impossible.

#Untrue.

#Lies.

Those people had no idea what they were missing.

I pull away. "But Totsie and I chat all day. Who am I supposed to talk to now?"

"Have an adventure. Write a letter."

"Letters take *forever*," I moan.

"You say that like such a letter expert." My mom shrugs, "Call her on daddy's old phone plugged into the wall. There is an entire world taking place off of computers. You're giving up being shut in a tiny bedroom in Baltimore for the chance to explore new worlds. Take it."

Grabbing Mr. Wibbles from the floorboard, I flop back in my seat and sigh, "I can't believe you're sending me to a place with no internet connection. Who does that?"

My mother reaches for my hand and squeezes. "I never promised wifi."

Chapter Three

The sound of crickets rises in the warm summer light as I step onto the dirt driveway. The smell of biscuits baking fills the air. Not the homemade kind. The ones from a can. Granddaddy knows how to cook canned biscuits, instant mashed potatoes, and peas in a can. The old farmhouse is enormous from the outside. Nothing like my apartment back home. Baltimore is a kitchen, bathroom, living room and bedroom all squeezed into one teeny square with walls.

Granddaddy is hunkered over the sink, digging something out of the drain when we walk inside. The screen door slams and makes him jump. Dark gray hair tumbles down over his forehead brushing gray stubble on his face. "Oh," he says, "you're early. A boy moved in next door with his father. I told him you'd be here today and he came around looking for you."

This is how it breaks down.

I am eleven years old.

Blue hair.

Crooked front tooth.

Smartest girl in my 6th-grade class.

Not much time for boys, next door or otherwise.

Granddaddy abandons the sink and walks over for hugs.

"Hi, daddy." My mom squeezes him tight.

"Big adjustment for all of us," Granddaddy says, eyeing me. "Come on upstairs. I got a room ready for you."

At the top of the wide, wooden staircase a heavy door swings easily into a bright room. Four poster bed, nightstand, and dresser. Sunlight streams over the dusty floor. It's the room we always stay in when visiting. The storage boxes have been removed. It looks more like a bedroom, less like a huge closet.

"Gosh," Granddaddy sighs in the doorway. "Time. It all goes somewhere, doesn't it? It can't possibly just disappear. I remember when this was your room," he says to Charlie Loop.

My mom's eyes sweep across the room. "So do I."

Silence falls over the Loops.

In the distance, a tractor rumbles across the fields. My mom glances out the window, then walks over, squinting. "What's going on out at that old burial mound."

Granddaddy wipes his hands on his jeans, twisting his mouth up the way he does when he's annoyed. "Some people from the university are digging out there. Looks like their funding finally came through."

"You okay with that?"

He shrugs. "It's always creepy when people start digging up bones and calling it research."

Burial mounds and my life being upended makes me blurt out, "Take me with you."

My mom looks at me. Granddaddy looks away.

19

Charlie Loop frowns and kneels down. "This is your home now."

"My home is in Baltimore. This was your idea."

"You're gonna have to say goodbye to Baltimore."

"I hate goodbye."

"You're going to have to find a way to love this place."

I throw my arms around my mom's neck and vow to never let go. I will never let go, I whisper inside my head repeatedly. I will never let go.

"You're acting like this is the last time we'll ever see each other," my mom says quietly.

I know all about *last* times.

The last blue raspberry Sno Cone me and Totsie shared.

The last time I saw my cartoon wall in my room.

The last time I saw my grandmother before she walked out into the fields and disappeared two years ago.

The last time I saw my father. In my room. In my home. In Baltimore.

"Look, why don't you go outside and meet the boy from next door?" My mom asks. "I need to talk with daddy alone. Okay? I promise this will all work out."

A fine line separates what you don't want to do from what you do. It's blurred with the pain of trying to make everyone happy.

Granddaddy eyes my glitter green combat boots and says, "Keep your boots on out there. This ain't the city."

No, it ain't the city, I think, backing away. Running down the staircase I whip around the corner and come face to face with a photo of my grandmother framed on the wall. I refuse to think about the last time. Not that time. Not again. The eyes in the photo are so real it makes my whole body shiver. She loved tunnels and drew them constantly. Pen and ink sketches of tunnels are framed up and down the wall. Big ones, small ones, ones with doors on either side. It feels like I'm being suffocated in tiny, dark drawings of places that don't exist. The hours come too fast, one after the other, leaving everything changed. I stare up into her eyes once more, heaving in a deep breath.

Chapter Four

A tiny, brown feather blows across the weathered boards of the back porch, coming to a stop in the corner. Stuck in a chipped piece of white paint it flutters in the breeze. I reach down but hesitate, my index finger suspended a foot away. It's always curious when dreams show up in waking hours. It doesn't happen often but the Loops have a history of life and dreams intersecting. I inhale deeply and pluck the feather out, holding it between finger and thumb.

"Hey," someone calls out.

I look up just in time to see a boy walking across the side yard. He's not a runt like boys back in middle school. From where I'm standing, I can see the roof of his house. It's not exactly close. Next door in the city means something totally different in the country. Quickly, I stuff the feather into my pocket.

Dusting hay off the front of his jeans, he says "Hey, my name is Rowan. Rumor has it you're going to be living here awhile." Turning, he stretches his arm and points, "I live over there with my dad. He's leading the team digging out at the mounds so I've been over here a lot."

"Granddaddy told me."

"So, what brings you out here?"

I shrug. Danger pay is my new vocabulary word. That's how change happens. Two words change my entire world. Two words send everyone speeding in a new direction. Two words equal one thing I don't even understand.

Kicking at rocks along the edge of wilted flowerbeds, I say, "My mom is going to Afghanistan."

Rowan's eyes widen. "That's really far."

"Only if you're counting the miles." I tear a dandelion out of the ground, close my eyes and blow its wispy pieces out in front of me, wishing this all away.

He shrugs. "True." He pauses, cocking his head. "So, what's your name?"

I squeeze my eyes shut, holding my wish tight. "Maya Loop."

"That's a cool name."

Trying to play off the compliment, I pinch my face up. "So how long have you been here?"

Rowan shrugs. "About six months. My dad works at the college in town."

Tips of tall wheat stalks hang under the weight of ripeness. An army of plants surround the yard.

Rowan leans in, confiding, "It's not as boring as you think."

Kicking a clump of dirt, I force a smile. "I kinda doubt it. It looks pretty boring."

"If you come out into the fields with me tonight, I'll show you the burial mound. I've been sneaking out there spying on my dad."

There is nothing I'd rather avoid more than the fields at night. They are menacing enough during the day with the endless sway that threatens to swallow me up. Dark fields full of skeletons is just about the most horrifying thing I can think of. I'll pass. Skip it. #NoWay. "That mound has been out there forever. Why is everyone suddenly so interested in it now?"

"The college thinks there might be important artifacts from a tribe of Indians that lived out here. I heard my dad talking. They had a prophet named Handsome Lake."

When I don't respond, he asks, "Are you afraid to go out there because of your grandmother?"

I eye him hard. "Why would you say that?"

Stepping back, Rowan shrugs, "I was just asking."

One night my grandmother walked out into those rows and was never seen again. Vanished. Even her footprints stopped like she was lifted straight into the air before she could take another step, like that mound swallowed her alive.

"Look, I'm not trying to be a jerk."

No one in B-more uses the word jerk. It's so outdated.

"I just want to show you something," he presses. "There are lights in the field, out by the mound. It's so freaking weird. I've seen them all week."

He holds up a pair of scuffed binoculars. "My room is on the second floor and I can see them from my house. It's too far away for me to figure out what they are. I'm going out there tonight. You could come with me."

Pointing at the binoculars, I slide into a smooth subject change, "Where'd you get those? Aren't they expensive?"

"I picked them up for a song at the thrift store in town."

Lifting a glitter green combat boot in the air, I say, "I got these at my favorite store back in Baltimore for ten bucks," because an awesome deal is an excellent distraction.

"Cool," he says.

No one says 'cool' anymore. I shrug. It's okay if he's dork boy.

A loud skittering sound kicks up from the bushes. The whole place is alive with creepy crawlies. Not like Baltimore. Like, scary alive. The fields at night are just about the most terrifying place in the world. I will not say that out loud to a boy I barely know. I've learned enough from boys back home not to admit weakness. They'll push you around on the concrete basketball courts and take whatever they can sell from your bag. Or the whole bag. Which is why I love my messenger bag so much. We've been through a lot. No one can ever really understand the loyalty between a girl and her messenger bag. #BagPower

Baltimore is never dark. Streetlights click on in the evening then click off when the sun breaks low over the water. An ache pushes into my gut. I miss that sunrise. Miss the shadows that follow me everywhere. Miss the takeout at Fong's Kitchen.

"So," he says, "wanna solve a mystery tonight?"

A mystery sounds better than staring at the ceiling without an internet connection but, "I don't think Granddaddy is going to let me go out that late."

Rowan tilts his binoculars left to right. "Don't tell him. Look, I'll watch from my house. I can see his window. When he goes to sleep, I'll come over and get you."

Shielding my eyes from the sun, I pretend to stare across the distance but really, I'm coming up with a good excuse. "I just got here," I start but that sounds silly so I aim for the truth. "I don't want to lie." Or go out in the dark to a burial mound, I finish in my mind. Dead people are so creepy.

Rowan raises his eyebrows in that way boys do when they think you will not take the dare. That look irks me to the core.

My mother yells from the front yard, "Maya?"

Rowan gives a nod and walks off, whispering over his shoulder, "I'll see you tonight."

Not likely, I think.

Chapter Five

Dinner is quiet. One lamp to illuminate a few spoken words. My grandmother's place is set across from mine. It's hard to watch Granddaddy wish for something I'm sure will never come even though I stare at the roses painted around the edge of her plate and wish for the same thing.

The caw of a crow echoes through the high ceilings. Granddaddy turns, looking over his shoulder, out the open window over the sink. A second later, cawing kicks up again.

"That's strange," he says, pushing his chair back from the table.

I know the sound. Crows pull trash from the cans along the waterfront.

Granddaddy turns in his chair to listen. "Unusual for them to be out at night. Downright weird, actually."

"Why?"

"Birds bed down for the night. Except for the big ones, owls and such. They come out to hunt."

I push warm buttered peas into my instant mashed potatoes with my fork and think about the blind sparrow. The feather I found on the porch is still in my pocket. Soft and small and hidden.

Granddaddy reaches for the floppy hat he still hooks on the back of grandmother's empty chair. "This might be cause for concern. Sometimes the coyotes sneak into the barn at night. You wait here. Things have been a little odd around here lately."

Waiting isn't my best subject.

Not by a long shot.

I drift over to look out the window. On the enamel sink top, my eyes stop on what looks like a tiny pair of goggles. Too small for a doll, it has pieces of gunk stuck to it from being in the drain. Gross and fascinating I poke at it with the tip of my finger.

After counting to ninety I creep into the shadows on the porch. A caw comes from the barn. I shiver. In all that darkness something catches my eye. A bright, magical flash of light in the fields. Horses stamp their feet and snort in the barn. The old boards of the back porch groan. My heart beats fast. Granddaddy doesn't like it when I'm headstrong and don't listen. Still, I lean over the railing watching the light, an effervescent spark dancing in-between the rows. My eyes flit across the wide-open space. The yard alone is massive compared to the tiny plot of grass in front of my apartment building back home. The lights move deeper into the fields of winter wheat. A dry *skeet skeet* noise kicks up, making my skin prickly.

One step.

Two step.

Barns are another world. The smell of horses and hay, the heavy scent of dry wood, grit, gravel.

Three step.

Dark skies stretch the entire length of the world. A warm glow from the barn spills into the yard. The shadow of Granddaddy flows smoothly across the wooden stalls. Leaning forward I watch him bend over as a crow hops backward. Picking something up from the ground, Granddaddy inspects it a moment before slipping it into his pocket. The crow cocks his head, watching, shiny black eyes glimmering in the barn light.

I watch from the barn door, breathing slowly, evenly. The crow backs up and catches sight of me. Every muscle in my body tenses when I realize I'm being watched. Yet, an unexpected reaction occurs. Instead of wanting to run, I look at the curves of his black feathers and think about drawing him when I get back upstairs.

Something deep and unsettling consumes my breath, threatening to swallow me up if I don't slip back through the screen door and take a seat at the table. Loops are like that. Constantly looking for clues, guided by their guts. I slip quietly back inside.

Granddaddy isn't far behind. Hooking his hat on the back of the chair he takes a seat. He lays his hand on the table like he's reaching for my grandmother's hand. The sight makes me a tad bit sad. Shadows of his fingers roll across the table. I miss her, too.

"What was it?" I ask.

"Some crows in the hayloft. Might have built a nest up there. Too dark to tell." He pulls a rusted gear out of his pocket and sets it on the table. "The crows were covering this up with hay."

A bright silver moon rises, positioned perfectly in the window. Stars fill up the room. In the silence, I hear scratching inside the walls. Granddaddy's eyes narrow. Tiny footsteps give me the creeps. I'd give just about anything for a bag of mini powdered doughnuts from the corner market back home.

No corner market.

No wireless.

No dial-up.

No mini powdered doughnuts.

I sigh really loud.

Granddaddy stares at the wall, brow furrowed. "I hope we don't have rats."

Chapter Six

The most technologically advanced piece of equipment in the entire house is the cordless phone. I adjust my messenger bag and make my way down the creaky stairs. Quietly, I take a seat on the wooden bench in the hall and dial. Each number beeps loudly so I stuff it inside my hoodie to muffle the sound. Positioning myself so I can see anyone coming I put the phone to my ear and listen. The house groans. Off in the kitchen, the sink drips. In-between every teeny sound the silence is a roar. I'm used to traffic and people yelling down the street. Hector and Marlo and Baby Squeaky.

The phone rings.

And rings.

I shift and fidget, tracing my fingers over tiny blue flowers on the wallpaper.

Landlines are so weird. Like ships that can't leave port. The phone is as big as my head.

A quiet voice says, "Hello?"

I sit straight up on the creaking bench. "Totsie?"

"Maya?"

"Yes," I whisper excitedly.

"Where are you?"

"At Granddaddy's farm. I called you this morning about a hundred times before I left."

"I had to go with Aunt Becky across town."

"Why?"

"I think mama's gotta go back to that place where they make her be alone."

Not the first time. The way I figure, it probably won't be the last, either. Totsie's mom is not my favorite person. Never has been. Totsie starts crying. At first, it sounds like a squeak but then she stumbles over words, sniffling.

"Hey, what's wrong?"

"I don't know," she stammers. "I know it's not the end of the world but it sure feels like it."

"You've been through this before."

"But I had you."

#truth #hurts

Big ups and downs were weathered together. Now we're far apart.

Totsie sniffles and sputters, "Do you like it there?"

"I've been here before."

"I mean, do you like living there?"

"It's dark and kinda creepy. Something was in the barn tonight."

"Like an animal?'

"I think it might have been in the walls, too."

32

There is a pause. Totsie sucks in a deep breath. "You should come back here. You can live in my room. My aunt won't care. She sleeps on the couch anyway."

I look down the long hall to the front door. On the other side of the glass, darkness swallows every living thing. To get back to Baltimore I will have to pick myself up and run through dark fields. It's unavoidable. I can get to a truck stop, beg a ride. I know I can get back to the city if I try.

After a long time, I say, "Maybe."

Totsie makes a little gaspy sound of glee. "I'll be here," she says.

Getting back home requires one blue-haired girl from Baltimore to become the brave I want to see in the world. My mother has a game called 'The Last One'. Instead of racing to be first, the two Loop girls grab the last cookie, the last drink, constantly angle to be the last person to say goodnight. Alpha to Omega, my mother always says. Open to close. Concept to completion. In a world of first place, I know the value of bringing something to a close. That's what bothers me the most about Charlie Loop being off in Afghanistan. It's all wide open. Beginnings and endings are all confused.

In my current mood, I'd hand over my thirty-three dollars' worth of allowance for one bag of powdered mini doughnuts.

Totsie whispers, "Do you think you can do it?"

33

That's like asking an astronaut if they think they can land on the moon. Of course, I can do it. Nodding like Totsie's actually in the room, I go on record. "Yes. I think I can."

"You think you can or you know you can?"

The million-dollar question.

The gentle sound of Granddaddy snoring can be heard through the floorboards. My eyes drift to the ceiling. Leaving is hard. It doesn't matter what I'm leaving, it feels hard. Leaving is the same as giving up.

"Argh," I groan. "I know I can. I just need to get a plan."

Totsie cheers far away. "Yay!"

"Okay, let me go upstairs and get my stuff. I'll report back later."

"Who rules the world?" Totsie asks.

I inhale sharply. The enormous task of getting back to Baltimore safely weighs heavily. Very quietly I say, "Girls do."

I hang up the phone but don't move. It's one thing to face a challenge, another thing to actually overcome it. Forcing myself to stand I walk to the bottom of the staircase. A noise on the landing gets my attention. Like a projection from an old movie camera, the image flickers and sputters. A faint image of my grandmother forms. Leaves and dirt cling to her clothes as she leans forward, yelling like she's trapped behind thick glass. The sight is so shocking I freeze, unable to look away. The urgency and fear in my grandmother's eyes make me back up. Except I forget I'm standing on the stairs and fall to the hardwood floor. The sensation of hitting bottom launches me forward as I struggle with my bag. The image fades out. Then my eyes shoot to the window at the end of the hall. The dark is everywhere. Framed sketches of tunnels line the walls. What I just saw can't be real. It can't. But that doesn't matter because I'm not staying in a house with a ghost.

Not now.

Not ever.

Chapter Seven

The dark shapes of winter wheat stand at the edge of the field, daring me to enter. The very fact that I'm going to have to leave the back porch squeezes my chest tight. The driveway leads back to the road but it will take hours. Cutting across the field is the fastest way to get to a truck stop. If I can get my body to actually step forward.

Do it, I whisper aloud.

Go now.

In the distance an owl hoots.

I've never heard a real owl. Only audio clips on nature cams.

Its voice is so loud and clear.

It must be a sign.

There is no part of me that wants to walk into the fields and yet the thought of going back upstairs terrifies me to the bone.

Sucking in a long breath, I adjust the straps on my messenger bag and run down the back steps before I can even think about what I'm really doing.

Clouds pass in front of the moon. I really want to be back in Baltimore. Upstairs, in my bedroom, staring at the glow of a chat screen.

Running is a maze. Pick a row. Run to the highway. Crops bump into other crops and the fields are bigger than they look from my bedroom window. Pushing all the nagging thoughts from my head I keep running, tripping on uneven ground. Getting back to the smooth sidewalks of Baltimore is my number one goal.

The smell of dirt is strong. I'm used to the smell of the ocean, still water at the docks. The smell of exhaust from buses and steamed buns from Fong's Kitchen. Even though I'm out for summer break it's still technically late spring. Rich earth rises up everywhere. Insects chirp and screech. Every time clouds pass in front of the moon shadows swallow me up. My messenger bag slaps against my leg, weighing down my shoulder. No time to stop and adjust.

Gotta go. Gotta go.

The pounding of my heart makes it impossible to catch my breath. It looked so simple from the window. Cross the fields to the open meadow, cut through the trees, to the highway on the other side. The wispy wheat plants slap my arms and face. The entire field sounds like fingernails on skin. Stalks scratching in the breeze.

Maybe it's a sign I should turn back.

Except blue-haired girls from Baltimore aren't quitters.

Turning back is not an option and yet I feel so turned around. The moon pops out from behind a cloud. Turning in a circle I hope to activate my inner compass. Back home my sense of direction is good. I can walk the entire neighborhood, eyes closed.

But these fields.

It's like another world.

I will be eaten by bears if I stand still. Lurching forward I head toward the next field over where stalks of corn rise up from the earth, freshly planted, only a few feet tall. Turning in a circle, I can't remember which way leads to the highway. I am so deep into the fields I can't see the farmhouse anymore. Turning in another circle I realize I have no idea where I am and I'm just going to have to follow a row.

Tiny spotlights flicker up from the ground. Rays of light wave through the dark as clouds sweep across the moon.

"What is that?" I whisper, leaning forward. "Hello?"

Footsteps pound down one of the rows. A light blinds me as I spin around.

"Who's there?" I yell, covering my face with my hands.

"It's me. I told you I'd come and get you. I've been on your back porch for half an hour."

"Have I been out here that long?"

"I don't know. Why didn't you wait for me?"

"My house is kinda weird right now. I think I saw a ghost."

"Serious?"

I drop my hands and nod. "I was about to walk up the stairs and I saw the ghost of my grandmother."

"That's creepy."

Inhaling sharp and quick, I say, "I've been hoping she was alive. If I saw her ghost then she's not alive, right? Anyway, I just don't want to stay in the house."

Rowan pauses then asks, "Did you see the lights?"

Happy for the subject change I admit, "I—well, I saw something."

Grabbing my hand, he pulls me off in another direction. "Come on. They always go toward the burial mound."

I want to tell him that I'm going back to Baltimore, but something deep in my gut says to keep quiet. If he knows where I'm going then he might try to stop me. I have to keep going.

"Do you have a camera?" he asks.

"An old one, yes."

"Does it work?"

I pinch my lips together. "Of course it works."

Streams of light flash up from the ground several rows over.

Rowan points, "Press record and follow me."

I bob and weave as I run down row after row of plants I can't even identify, videotaping with one hand, waving the other to the side to maintain balance.

Rowan is breathless. "I told you."

Up ahead lights wave in the air then turn swiftly into a different row and disappear from sight. I lean over to get a better look. Suddenly, the lights dash by, several rows over, moving in the opposite direction.

"Run," Rowan stumbles over rows of dirt.

I take a huge breath. Not a lot of fields back in Baltimore. Rowan crashes through the stalks. Squeezing the camera tight in one hand, I use the other to push thick green leaves out of the way. Light

39

bursts up from the ground, brilliant and bright against the dark sky. A gasp falls from my mouth. Lights dance to and fro with a jerking motion. The soft earth gives under my feet as I run closer. Lights swoop around and disappear over the burial mound.

I stand still, waiting for the lights to rise. The full moon pushes high into the sky. My camera moans and powers down as the battery craps out.

"Did you see that?" Rowan bursts through a row of green stalks. "I am not crazy. My dad thinks I am totally crazy." His huge eyes sparkle in the moonlight. "What do you think they are? I thought they were fireflies but they can't be."

"How many times have you seen these lights?"

His eyes trail upwards, thinking. "A lot. Especially since they started digging out here."

"Could these be lightning bugs?"

Rowan's brow pinches up. "Kinda big for bugs but my dad has all kinds of books on insects. Let's watch the footage, see if we can identify anything."

"We can't. My battery died. I need to plug it in."

Rowan groans. "Alright. Come on. I think my house is closer."

Standing there in the dark, clutching my camera, I think about telling him I'm going back to Baltimore. Keeping secrets is hard. Totsie can keep a secret, not me.

"Hey, do you have the internet?" I yell.

Rowan laughs. "You're in the country, not the year 1982. Don't be an ignoramus."

Chapter Eight

On a round, wooden table in the center of the office sits a big jar. Next to the jar, a pair of funny glasses sits on top of a case. Rowan turns on a lamp. As my eyes adjust to the light, I hear a faint scratching. A desperate sound. Urgent. Frantic, yet so incredibly light. My eyes sweep around the room and stop on the jar. That's when I see it isn't an ordinary jar nor is it empty.

"Someone is trapped," I say.

Rowan smacks his head on the bottom of a shelf. "What? Where?"

I point to the table. Inside the jar is a large bug. "What is that?" I walk closer, staring straight through the glass. Totsie loves bugs. She will talk me into scooping any bug up with my hands.

Rowan's face turns serious, the corners of his lips pull into a frown. "That's the Killing Jar," he says softly.

"The what?"

"Dad puts specimens in the jar and seals it. They run out of air."

The truth settles over me in a prickly way. Pulling back from the jar my eyes shoot to dozens of picture frames on the walls full of dead insects. Spotted wings, long black bodies, glassy eyes, and polished legs.

"He suffocates the bugs?"

Rowan raises an eyebrow. "The butterflies, the crickets, the praying mantis." He sucks in a huge breath and confides, "They know they're dying. It's awful."

"What kind of bug is that?" I point to the jar.

"It's an Assassin Bug."

"Is it poisonous?"

"It's kind of like a Shield bug or a Stink bug. Pretty rare around here. I've never actually seen one. While the name suggests otherwise, I'm pretty sure they're harmless."

The Assassin Bug lays his front legs on the glass, pleading.

"We can't just leave him there," I say. "He'll die."

"My dad will freak out if I let one of his specimens go."

A shiver makes my spine tremble. *Specimen.* Not a real life-form, an experiment. I don't want Rowan to get in trouble. The world is a small place, the town even smaller. Still, the thought of walking away from a living being while it suffocates is beyond horrible. *Who just kills things?* That's why we left Baltimore. The city is so dangerous that people in my apartment building were killed. Dead on the streets, in abandoned warehouses. It's all over the news.

The Assassin Bug looks up at the lid. My eyes sweep around the room at dead bugs on the walls. Insects that laid their hands desperately against the glass and begged to live.

Rowan grabs a thick book about bugs and walks into the hall. "Come on. We'll check this book and see if there are any kind that might emit light but I kind of doubt it."

I lay a finger against the jar and whisper, "I will come back for you."

"*If you do, I will ring the bell,*" a voice whispers.

I pull my hand from the glass.

"What are you doing," Rowan huffs from the hallway.

"Did you hear that?"

Rowan shakes his head, casting shadows over the walls. "Come on. We're not supposed to be in here."

"*He can't hear me,*" the voice says.

I spin around. The house is perfectly quiet except for my heartbeat pounding in my ears. I lock eyes with the Assassin Bug.

"*Please come back for me,*" the voice says. "*I don't have much air left.*"

Chapter Nine

Rowan's bedroom walls are covered with posters. Mostly UFOs and dinosaurs. Dirty clothes are tossed all over the floor. I navigate around a pair of jeans and a wadded-up tee. He plops down on the rug and plugs the charger cord into the outlet, the other end into the camera.

Outside the window, the farmhouse glows in the distance. Faint light of the moon slants off the roof when the clouds part. It feels so far away. Like the rest of my life. The camera whirs, the tiny screen flickers. Rowan leans forward excited and presses rewind.

Solving the mystery of the lights should be pressing. In fact, I've never let anyone touch my camera but I can't stop thinking about the bug. It's down there dying while we're hunched over a screen. It's hard to focus when someone is running out of air in the other room.

"Here," Rowan whispers, pointing.

In the rush to get footage I forgot to switch to night vision. All I can make out is faint moonlight reflecting off the tips of leaves. Suddenly light flashes on the screen.

Sounds of scratching invade the room, making my skin crawl. I know it's the bug, scratching for his life. I watch Rowan.

His eyes are glued to the screen. The fact that he can't hear the scratching is weird.

"Look." He presses pause.

Leaning forward I stare at the screen. The lights appear to come out of the ground like mini spotlights.

"What do you think these are from?"

Scratch. Scratch.

"I don't know," I answer honestly, "but there's definitely something there."

Leaning back, he rubs his chin like characters in movies. He's so deep in thought he doesn't notice me concocting a plan. Outside the window, clouds pass in front of the moon darkening the room. Rowan presses play again. Lights flash, then several seconds of dark screen, the sound of breathing and yelling back and forth in the fields.

Scratch. Scratch.

Lights pop up and bob. Rowan presses pause again and we hunker down, head to head, staring at the screen.

"Where are they coming from?"

I point to the edge of the burial mound. "It looks like they're coming straight out of the ground."

"Except that can't be possible. Light doesn't just shoot out of the ground."

Because I'm a practical blue-haired girl, I shrug and say, "That we know of."

"There isn't much time left," whispers the voice downstairs.

Before I can lose my nerve, I announce the best lie I can concoct on the fly. "I have to use the bathroom."

There is just enough light to see the frown on his face. "Seriously?"

"Yes," I scowl. A scowl perfected in Baltimore because boys there are totally scowl worthy even if it is an old fuddy-duddy word.

"Okay, you've got to go back downstairs because the bathroom up here is right next to my dad's room."

Score.

"The stairs creak. Be quiet."

A winning wiggle propels me out to the landing. At the bottom, I stop to listen. Behind me the camera motor whirs. A spider web glints in the moonlight. The faint sound of scratching trails down the hall. Taking a deep breath, I walk straight for the killing jar.

The Assassin Bug turns, watching me walk through the door. Without hesitation, without jostling, I unscrew the lid and gently lay the jar on its side.

The Assassin Bug stumbles out, chest heaving.

"Go on," I whisper, setting the jar upright and screwing the lid back on. "Get out of here before he comes down and puts you back in that awful jar."

The Assassin Bug looks up at me in the moonlight. The strange features of his face make him seem human and alien at the same time. The floor creaks overhead.

I touch him from behind, worried about stingers on a bug with such an ominous name. "There's a window in the kitchen that's open. I saw it on the way in. Go. And never come back here again."

I have never been in trouble. Not with teachers or parents or police, and I will not start by getting caught in the act of setting bugs free. Quietly, I tiptoe across the hall to the bathroom, flush the toilet to keep up my cover and take the stairs two at a time.

Rowan's face is full of suspicion. "What took you so long?"

"I didn't want to turn on the lights." Quick subject change. "Did you figure out what's in the fields?"

"No, but I found this." Pointing at the screen he presses play. Shadows move across the screen.

"What is that?"

"I don't know but I saw it in the fields a few days ago. Like giant shadows."

"Where are they coming from?"

"The burial mound."

"Man, that thing is creepy."

"Yeah. I saw a bunch of shadows. Then I saw a man go into the dirt who never came out."

I don't want to say it out loud, but I'm only as strong as the fear I face. "My grandmother's footsteps ended at the burial mound."

"I thought she was lost in the fields?"

I shake my head. "She walked out into the fields but Granddaddy and the farm hands tracked her to the mound. Her footprints just stopped."

Rowan pulls his lips tight. "People in town say she didn't disappear."

"Then where did she go?"

Holding his lips tight, his cheeks fill with air. Exhaling, he says, "I've just heard people talking."

"About?"

He shrugs, turning his attention back to the camera to avoid my glare. "That maybe she didn't disappear. Maybe something happened to her."

"Like she got eaten by bears?"

He laughs unexpectedly and covers his mouth, mumbling, "We don't have bears out here."

"You're stalling. Tell me what you heard."

"Some people in town think your granddaddy might have killed her."

A queasy, uneasy feeling grips me tight. "What?" Falling back on my heels to steady myself, I crouch next to him on the rug. "He would never do anything like that."

Suddenly, the unfamiliar room with the unfamiliar boy, in the unfamiliar house, makes me extremely uncomfortable. Like the world is closing in. Like I'm the one inside the killing jar.

Rowan folds the LCD screen until it locks in place. "I'm just telling you because you're alone. Maybe you should lock your door at night just in case."

That thought never occurred to me. Ever. I've always assumed in the back of my mind that one day they'll find my grandmother, lost, wandering the streets unable to remember her name or her former life. It happens to people in movies all of the time. Amnesia. But seeing her ghost on the stairs makes me lose hope in that dream.

Maybe she is gone.

Maybe something did happen.

"You can stay here during the day. My dad is gone. He spends all of his time at the college or at the burial mound."

"Maybe," I say slowly, to acknowledge the offer. Adjusting my messenger bag, I tuck my camera inside. "It's late. I have to go."

Rowan stands up and I realize we are the same height.

"I didn't mean to freak you out. I just heard my dad talking to people in town. I thought you should know."

"It's okay," I say, quietly turning to leave.

"I wasn't trying to be a jerk."

"No one says jerk anymore."

***

The walk back to the farmhouse is long. Everything is stacked on top of everything else in B-more. People, apartment buildings, businesses, satellite dishes, rooftop gardens in the expensive joints that line the waterfront. Out here all this space is a lot wider than it appears. Stumbling over dirt clods reminds me how much I miss smooth sidewalks. To pass the time I imagine what I will say to Totsie when we see each other. It's going to be all smiles and *OMG, high five, hug hug and listen girl, I saw a ghost.* Totsie will freak out. Seeing a real ghost is her number one goal. Countless hours passed with us staring at ghost videos online. Now her best friend has actually seen one. On second thought, maybe I should just go straight to the highway. I stop and look out over the fields. Maybe I should just hoof it to a gas station. My glitter green combat boots are ready for adventure.

A light clicks on inside the farmhouse. That can only mean one thing. Granddaddy is up. The light is in my room. From where I'm standing, I can make out the shape of my unpacked suitcase on the dresser. Dang. Now I'm exhausted, wet, still not back in Baltimore and in trouble to top it off.

Out on that dusty piece of earth, I stare at the glowing window. I have no choice. Now I have to march into that house and demand Granddaddy drive me back to Baltimore.

I'm not sleeping a single night in a house with ghosts. Nope. Not this blue-haired girl. No way, no how. Certainly not sleeping a single night in a house with the person who may have turned my grandmother into a ghost. Suddenly the wide-open space and dark sky overwhelm my senses. A big sigh heaves up my chest. I will tell him what those people in town are saying. I will tell him, whether he likes it or not.

51

Chapter Ten

Pausing at the bottom of the stairs to catch my breath, I hear the gentle sounds of snoring on the second floor. That's weird. *If he's asleep, then who turned on the light?* Looking for ghosts I take the first step. Sensing something behind me I whip around but the hall is empty. Or it looks empty. But I know from watching all those scary movies with Totsie that ghosts can be invisible. With my heart pounding, I try to calm down and come up with options. To get to the second floor, I must go up the stairs.

If Granddaddy isn't awake the ghost *must* have turned on the light. The very thought terrifies me more than the apartment elevator that jams in-between floors. I think about all the haunted places back in Baltimore. The old lot behind the school haunted by a little boy who took a dare and died. The abandoned brick building that faces the market. The one that a woman haunts by walking up and down the crumbling staircase of the Canton Grain elevator. Shivers flitter down my arms. Blue-haired girls from Baltimore don't dig the dark, dirt or creepy ghosts. Even if we are related.

Cresting the top of the stairs, I am surprised to see my bedroom door closed. That can only mean one thing. The ghost is in my room. Every cell in my body demands I turn around and walk out to the main road to find a ride home. But I've never been one to turn down a dare. Ever.

It takes a lot of courage, but finally I tiptoe down the hall and quietly turn the knob. Slowly, I open the door and step inside. The light is on but my room is empty. Confused, I lean back and sneak a peek down the hall. If I stand very still, I can hear the gentle sound of Granddaddy snoring. My imagination is off the charts. Shaking off my suspicion I walk over and plug my camera in to charge.

Someone clears their throat. I spin around. The Assassin Bug stands in the middle of the room. I wonder how he got here because that's a curious distance for a bug to travel even with super long legs.

The Assassin Bug looks up. "A series of underground tunnels. You?"

I step backward, raising my chin, glancing around. Bugs don't talk. That's totally nutso. There must be someone else in this room.

The Assassin Bug huffs out loud. "No one says nutso anymore."

Lowering myself to the rug, resting on my elbows, I come face to face with the weird bug. "Did you just read my mind?"

"I prefer the term insect, but we really haven't time to discuss specific word choices."

Without blinking, I acknowledge his request, "Wait a minute. I heard you back at Rowan's house. That was you, in the jar."

The Assassin Bug smiles. An honest-to-goodness insect smile. "Yes, you did. That is why we chose you. You're a very smart girl."

The compliment is nice, but I'm onto the next question. "That's all fine and good, but if you can talk and read minds, then how did you land yourself up in that killing jar?"

The Assassin Bug rises up on his hind legs, dusting himself off. "I'll have you know I was on the roof of the barn, waiting for your arrival and I fell onto a pile of dirt. Right next to that killer. Quite the mistake, I admit."

"Are you talking about Rowan's father?"

"None other than Thomas Tannebaum, himself. Insect-hater extraordinaire."

"So, you can read minds, but not predict the future?"

"Exactly. That's what we need you for."

"Because I can predict the future?"

"Because you will save the future."

Big talk for a bug. "How can I save the future?"

He extends a long, skinny hand in my direction. "Come with me."

The glowing moon peeks from behind thick clouds, sparkling along the windowsill. "I haven't checked lately, but I am pretty sure I'm not supposed to go out with strange bugs late at night."

"You may think this is funny but there is a great war going on, one that humans cannot see. A war with the Landions, who want to turn back the clock to the day before your kind ever existed."

I feel around for the soft feather in my pocket, to make sure I'm not dreaming. "What are you talking about?"

The Assassin Bug lifts his brow, making his antennae wiggle. "The Landions don't just want to kill you. They want to make sure you never existed."

I lay my palms on the floor and shake my head fiercely. "No. That can't be done. That's impossible. This is just some ridiculous story you made up."

"Oh, it can be done, and if it weren't for myself and a few others, it would be done. Humans think of time as a progression, linear, something that goes backward and forward. But time is an element, a sort of building block of the world, and it can be extinguished, like fire."

"You're saying humans can be removed?"

The Assassin Bug nods. "Not just removed. Erased."

"But why would a thing like that even exist?"

"To keep the balance of all worlds. But times are dark now, and it's used for power and control."

I push myself up from the floor. Standing tall, I say— perhaps too loudly, "I don't believe you." My eyes glance around the bare walls of my room and stop on the strange bug I freed from the killing jar.

The Assassin Bug exhales quietly. "They will come."

Curious lights flicker inside a tiny mousehole in the baseboard. Like the lights in the fields. Suddenly, there's a lot of scratching and grunting, then the sound of tiny footsteps. I watch a squadron of moles wearing aviator goggles file out of the mousehole. One after the other they come, forming a motley line. Seven sets of seven shuffling into wobbly formation.

The Assassin Bug whispers, "They call your people the uprights."

Two moles walk to the front holding spears. One carries a clipboard. The latter salutes with his wide palm and furry hand.

Kneeling down for a better look, I lay my hands on my knees and ask, "What's with the funny goggles?"

"They help us assemble time particles. You can't rearrange a particle until you assemble it first," the saluting mole answers. "Plus, it helps us see better. It's dark down there."

The lights on their heads flash across the ceiling, reminding me of only one thing. "You were the lights in the fields, weren't you?"

Lights bob all around the walls as the moles nod.

"What were you doing in the fields," the Assassin Bug interrupts.

The mole looks down at the clipboard, flips through a few pages, and says, "You told us she loves the fields."

"I told you that she's afraid of the dark."

"Stop talking about me like I'm not in the room." It is one thing to fear the dark, and quite another to be made to look like a baby in front of a bunch of moles wearing aviator goggles. "Why didn't you tell me all this when I let you out of the jar?"

The Assassin Bug pulls his mouth into a flat smile. "Hardly the conversation to have in front of the human boy, don't you think?"

"You rang?" another mole asks, abruptly.

I turn to a mole with a spear. "I did?"

"The bell," the mole with the clipboard says, matter-of-factly.

There are many bells in my life. The bell on my bicycle, alone in the storage unit back home. The school bell. The bell that rings at Fong's Kitchen when my sweet and sour chicken is ready for pickup.

"I rang the bell," the Assassin Bug says.

Seven sets of seven moles turn. "*You* rang?"

The Assassin Bug nods.

"Only an upright can ring the bell," the mole with the clipboard says, confused.

All the moles turn to leave.

"Wait!" the Assassin Bug commands.

The mole in front stops, causing the ones behind him to bump into a pile.

"This upright is the only one left. She doesn't know how to ring the bell."

The moles look me up and down, eyes lingering on my scrawny arms.

"Take her to see the Orb Weaver. She will give permission," the Assassin Bug states.

The moles smooth their fur and huddle together, whispering.

The conversation is weird enough, what with the talking bugs and moles, but no one in my family has ever mentioned being summoned. This makes me nervous. I'm pretty sure they're in the wrong place. Maybe I fell in the field and hit my head.

"This must be a mistake," I blurt out. "I'm from Baltimore. You have to be talking about someone else."

The Assassin Bug glances out of the corner of his eye, and says in a rather stern voice, "We know exactly who we're talking about."

With a blue-haired brain full of protests, I express none because something deep in my gut feels like a magnet, drawn to the situation. It's so late, almost dawn. Granddaddy wakes early. I don't want him to find me talking to a large, odd-looking bug, and seven sets of seven moles, all wearing aviator goggles and lights strapped to their heads. Some things are hard to explain. This might be harder than others.

The moles shake their heads. Lights dance across the ceiling. "The upright must ring the bell."

"You won't help her?"

"Rules are rules," the mole shrugs.

"We have no time for this." The Assassin Bug waves the moles away. "Put me on your shoulder," he says to me. "We must go."

I swoop down so he can march onto the palm of my hand. It's an ominous moment and I wonder if he will sting.

The moles march back into the hole. "Down from below, all good things come."

"Follow them," the Assassin Bug points.

I pinch my face up funny and tight. "Umm, I can't fit through that hole."

"Draw a door," the Assassin Bug instructs.

"What?"

"With your sketch pad and pen, draw a door."

I have carried the sketchpad since my dad died but never once opened it. Flipping through my dad's work is a reminder he's gone. Sure, I carry it everywhere, but the pages are untouched.

"How do you know about my dad's sketchpad? Have you been spying on me?" Impatient bugs are the worst, I think, reaching deep into my bag.

"Everyone knows about the prophecy of the Loops. Now draw a door."

Chapter Eleven

Everything goes black. The sound of a match striking stone makes me jump. A flame sputters, flickers and takes hold. I look down. At my feet, the Assassin Bug holds a wooden match as big as his body.

Pointing up, he instructs, "Help me with the lantern."

Glass lanterns on hooks line the stone walls. Carefully, I take the match before it burns down. After lighting the wick, I replace the glass cover. "Where are we?"

The earth trembles. Flecks of dirt land on my shoulder. Beetles skitter to and fro in the light. The flame sputters.

"The Landions have been collapsing all of the doorways in and out of your world. This is one of the only shortcuts left. The beetles show their displeasure by grumbling."

The clicks, chirps and *tatatata* sounds of insects are magnified.

Blue-haired girls from B-more don't really dig the dirt. "It feels like we're going to be swallowed alive."

"The Landions certainly would love to swallow us up but they were locked out of the tunnels long ago. Come along."

At the end of the tunnel I step into a long hall with doors on either side. The dark hallway extends, then curves, a long, twisty spiral that makes me dizzy.

I stare down at the simple door I drew on a blank page. A rectangle with a knob. I can't really draw. At least, not like my dad. I'm not sure what I just did so I stuff my sketchpad deep into my bag, holding onto the edges a few seconds longer. After adjusting the strap, my stomach growls. "I should have packed a lunch," I say, pausing to consider the fact that I've neither eaten nor slept.

"That will not be necessary," the Assassin Bug says hastily. "There will be no time to eat."

Shadows rise over my shoulder as I follow the Assassin Bug down a set of crumbling steps. "All is well," he says confidently.

I'm not so sure. The only thing worse than the dark is being surrounded by dirt. Fears of being smothered grip me tight and make my heart beat fast. Dark, teeming earth seethes around me. Earthworms push their way through mounds of dirt along the path. Under the surface, a hidden world thrives.

"Press onward," the Assassin Bug urges, holding his tiny torch.

Down we go, my feet on crumbling dirt, curving to the right, then left.

The earth rumbles. Chunks of dirt land on my shoulders.

A little more frantic than usual, I ask, "Is this an earthquake? Should we get out?"

"You're going to have to get used to danger."

Stealing a glance back through the tunnel of dirt, not a single ray of light shines. Darkness on top of darkness in ways that make my skin shiver.

At the end, I step into a long hall with doors on either side. It looks like the abandoned subway stations we used to sneak down into back in Baltimore. But these tunnels have big doors with metal hinges. Hundreds of hallways with hundreds of doors, all stretching out as far as my eyes can see. Each door is different, all perfectly spaced up and down. Some are wood, some metal, even colored glass. I lay my hand on a knob, sure we are about to enter one of the rooms.

"You must never open these doors," he snaps.

I pull my hand away. "Why not? Are they bad?"

"You create your own door. If you enter through someone else's door you enter a different timeline and change everything."

The Assassin Bug rounds the corner at the end of the hall. I hurry to catch up. A breath catches in my throat when I step into a huge, cavernous room. Old lamps on posts, burning oil. Before me, an underground river reflects flickering light. The Assassin Bug walks quickly to a small rowboat. Wooden oars carved with mystic knots sit on the seats in the middle of the boat.

Scurrying up the side, he calls out, "We really must hurry. Being trapped in that jar set us back a bit."

The silence and stillness underground are incredible, even breath returns an echo. The soft thump of my glitter green combat boots in the cave-like room sounds foreign and odd. The boat tips dangerously to the side as I step in. The Assassin Bug holds tight to a wooden oar. "Easy now."

I grip the stern, balancing. Then, with great force, I push the boat from the stone steps. There is a split-second feeling when a boat swooshes out from land. A feeling of flying, gliding across the surface, setting off on a new adventure.

"How long will we be gone?" I ask, worried. Totsie will be counting the seconds. I'm supposed to be on the road to Baltimore.

"Life is a rhythm, not a schedule."

Okay, I can get behind that slogan. If we hurry. Water ripples as I cut through a liquid too dark and deep to contemplate.

The Assassin Bug points to a huge tunnel, "That way. The Orb Weaver will be waiting."

The boat rushes swiftly toward an opening that looks like a wide mouth ready to eat us alive.

Chapter Twelve

The river flows past lanterns hooked to the stone walls. Water slaps the tunnel walls, echoing back. I row the boat, scraping the sides when the tunnel narrows, then widens. Around each corner the river continues on. The doors are just as endless. Each one illuminated for seconds as we pass. It's the crumbling doors that make me worry. The ones falling apart or caving in. The ones too old to ever open again.

"Where do all of these doors lead?"

The Assassin Bug's eyes sweep past a bronze door with shiny, etched symbols of the moon, to a plain wooden one, warped with wear and buckling at the corners.

"These doors all lead to different times. Time so old, it is forgotten. Other doors to times you haven't known."

"Created by people?"

"Time is independent of humans. Humans are but one small addition to a much larger number of life."

"So where do they all lead?"

"They can, in truth, lead to infinity. Doors to doors to doors. Time branching into timelines that never end."

A carved red door comes into view, followed by a door so old dirt has filled the front.

The Assassin Bug tilts his head. "Some timelines end."

That's the saddest thing I've ever heard. "Why would some go so far and others end?"

"It is the question we all ask of everything. I suppose it is the tenacity of life to be so mysterious and yielding. Everything so fragile and resilient. Just when a timeline looks like it has to end it can suddenly branch off in a new direction."

I understand. It's the same feeling I get when I'm riding my bike down a side street but then suddenly, without reason, jerk the handlebars and take off across an empty lot. That moment of freedom colliding with unfamiliarity. That moment when I am certain I can ride forever, and if I ride fast enough then I can fly.

"Why are all of these doors down here?"

"Because that is how your world was organized. The original clock of the world was a water clock. An enormous, magnificent contraption. When it was dismantled the water flowed out and time became a river. It's been that way ever since. The moles dug the original tunnels and became the keepers."

The way my voice echoes is soothing, though my arms are aching from rowing. "So what is all of this? Where does it lead? I never knew there was a river under the farm."

"The river is under everything."

"Where does it go?"

"Back and forth across forever."

"That's a really long river."

"That's just how it shows up in your world."

"What is it then?"

"Time."

"Do you mean like time on a clock?" Glancing around, I let the oars skim the surface. "You mean we're traveling on time? Right now?"

"Time is the great organizer. Onward it flows."

"What if we get lost?"

"Time is never lost."

"Then where are we?"

"We are trying to find a short cut. It took your people a long time to realize the prophecy is real. I have to figure out a way to get you across the River of Great Divide without being caught. The fastest way to do that is to weave you into a timeline. Your grandmother was very smart and managed to do a lot before she was captured by the Landions."

The oars become heavy, sliding from the loosening grip of my palms. Into the dark water they go without a splash. More like a swallow. The boat sways, the front knocking into the stone wall on the left. "How do you know about my grandmother?" My voice echoes over and over. *Grandmother grandmother grandmother…*

The Assassin Bug holds his position on the wooden seat though the boat rocks. The outline of his strange body is etched in shadows on the wall. "Maybe I've said too much."

"Oh, no you don't," I say. "You can't back out. Tell me what you're talking about."

"I will help you," he states in a serious, even tone, "but we must keep going. There is another set of oars fastened to the side."

"Where is she?"

"I don't know exactly. I don't even know if she is still alive. I only know that she was captured. Everything is a guess at this point. The Landions have a huge advantage over you. If they rebuild the original clock then they reset time. Only one piece of the clock is now missing. As soon as they have it in hand, the clock will be rebuilt."

"Who took it apart?"

"The clock was dismantled a long time ago. The pieces were hidden across all worlds. We think the Reclamation Specialists may have had something to do with it but we can't be sure."

"And you think my grandmother is a part of this?"

The Assassin Bug nods, "The Landions believe your grandmother found the last piece before they could get to it and she hid it once more."

"Did she really find the piece?"

The Assassin bug looks at me, unblinking. "Yes, she did."

"Tell me where she is."

"What do you think we're doing? Get the oars."

Reaching to the side I tip the boat dangerously. Throwing my weight backward to regain balance I fall, scraping my arm.

"Ouch," I yell.

67

"HELP!"

"What?" Pushing upright I look inside the boat. The lantern swings on its hook, throwing shadows all over the tunnel, making me dizzy.

"HELP!"

Following the sound, I roll to the other side and look over the edge. The Assassin Bug flails in the water. Gulping for air, he reaches up but sinks. The river flows, knocking the boat against the stone wall. Grabbing at the surface, I hesitate then plunge my hand into the dark, cold water. The Assassin Bug grabs my finger.

Even though I expect the sensation, I let out a gasp. Pulling my hand out of the water I see the Assassin Bug, all legs wrapped around my fingers. Water drips from his body as I set him on the wooden bench.

"There is no time to stop," he doubles over, catching his breath. "Every moment we have is borrowed by staying one step ahead."

One step ahead is a game back in B-More.

The moles file out of a small hole in the tunnel wall, lights flashing wildly, crisscrossing over the ceiling.

I've never been so happy to see seven sets of seven moles in all my life. "Oh, my," one of the moles says.

The Assassin Bug straightens himself upright. "Thank goodness you've come to help."

Another mole shakes his head. "The uprights aren't supposed to be down here and you aren't supposed to be helping. It is strictly against the rules."

"Bug off," I say, using an oar to push off from the side. "I got this."

Chapter Thirteen

After what feels like hours of rowing, I spot a rusted metal pole set in stone steps. Shadows flicker along the walls like dark monsters dancing.

"Tie the boat off here," the Assassin Bug says, pointing at the pole.

The boat bumps against the wall as he hops to my hand and clamors up the stone to the path. "Come along now," he says, walking past several doors.

Totsie and I spent a lot of time at the docks watching the workers. Tying the rope like a pro, I steady the boat enough to hoist one leg onto the stone steps. Pulling the oars inside, I use them to steady myself. The boat wobbles with indecision.

The Assassin Bug points up at a plain brown door with a spider web spun across the top corner. "This one," he says. "Help me get it open."

A blinding light assaults my eyes when the door opens. After a few seconds, I'm able to squint. A huge meadow stretches to the horizon. It looks like the golf courses back home on the other side of town. Cranes fly above, chattering to each other in the air. Blue sky rolls into a lush green meadow. It's so different after being underground.

The Assassin Bug scrambles up my arm to perch on my shoulder.

"How did we get from way down there to up here?" I swallow back the unfamiliar quiver in my voice.

"It's called an 'overlap'. We go down to go up."

"Okay," I say slowly, "what exactly does that mean?"

"It means I can see the seams where points in time overlap. All insects can move through time. Humans see differently. And for you, everything is not what it seems."

"It seems like humans can't see a lot," I admit, self-consciously.

The Assassin Bug leads me across the grass. "Well, your kind certainly doesn't have the intelligence of an insect."

Touchy subjects require a change of topic. "Who is the Orb Weaver?"

Looking left, then right, trying to remember which way, "The Orb Weaver is the only one who can weave someone into a timeline."

A great shudder sweeps across the meadow, like heatwaves rippling over a long stretch of asphalt in the middle of summer. A second later an elevator pushes up through the earth and appears. One loud ding occurs as the doors slide open. Seven sets of seven moles march into the pale, shimmering light.

One mole asks, "Who ordered the elevator?"

The Assassin Bug pinches his face tight. "Not now," he instructs. "Besides, we could have used a ride."

The mole shakes his head. "Rules are rules."

In the middle of the meadow a great web unfolds in golden light. A blue spider with diamond eyes climbs out to the center. "What have you done?"

Seven sets of seven moles all turn at once and point to me. I pinch my face up, awkwardly, and act like they're nutso. I kick at the ground with my glitter green combat boots and try to avoid eye contact. Large insects are scary, especially when they talk. Trust me on this.

The spider squints, then shakes his head. "Uprights? Here? No way. No how. There is nothing I can do for her. The Landions have spoken."

The Assassin Bug leaps into the tall grass, marching forward. "That cannot be. The Landions are not the final authority."

"Can be. Will be." The spider waves his legs dismissively. "Humans had their chances. Too many to count. Leave before trouble kicks up."

"We must see the Orb Weaver."

A great breeze blows. Air swirls through the web.

The blue spider grips the fine threads tightly, tossed about. "No."

One of the moles yells, "To the elevator!"

The Assassin Bug looks away from the spider. When he sees the great swirling, his mouth falls open and he screams, "RUN!"

Scrambling in a panic, he waves. The moles clutch their spears upright and make a wobbly dash for the elevator that stands all by itself, attached to absolutely nothing. I stare at the shiny metal walls. Too big to be an optical illusion I watch, mesmerized, as moles tumble inside.

The Assassin Bug stumbles through the grass. "Run. Run now, or it's all over."

Suddenly, huge patches of earth rise up. A hissing, ticking sound seeps into the air. Enormous figures, the color of dirt, rise twenty feet tall. Bulging, wrathful eyes, and sharpened teeth. Helmets that look like giant beetle skulls. They're everywhere, and they seem to run straight toward me. Back in Baltimore, things like this happen in video games when me and Totsie are left alone and told never to answer the door. We hide in chair forts and climb level after level until the potato chip bag is empty. I am not in Baltimore anymore. That is very clear.

The Assassin Bug runs up my leg and holds onto my shoulder. The sensation makes me shake him off. Bugs holding onto me are not a #squadgoal. The huge, dirt-colored giants run, making the air swirl horribly.

The Assassin Bug screams, tumbling to the ground, "We have to RUN!" The sudden shrillness of his voice breaks my trance. This is not a video game. This is my life. Which, I will point out, has officially become weirder than a video game. The elevator doors start to close. One mole, then another, then another, jumps forward

73

to hold the doors open. Lots of grunting and pushing, goggles knocked to and fro.

I snatch up the Assassin Bug, put him on my shoulder, and sprint the way my coach back in 6th Grade Phys Ed taught. Lurching forward, I pry open the doors and squeeze in sideways. A hand comes down on my shoulder. The doors are almost closed. I throw my weight forward and fall into the elevator. The moles grunt. I spin around as the doors close and have just enough time to see the Assassin Bug squeezed tight in the hand of one giant, hissing monster.

"The green scarab will lead you home," the Assassin Bug yells frantically.

"What?" I yell.

The doors close in my face.

"No," I scream.

Moles pound their spears on the elevator floor.

The elevator lurches into its descent. Music clicks on, easy and smooth. Down the elevator goes. Down into the earth.

Searching desperately for a stop button, I yell, "We have to help him …" my voice trails off as I realize the panel is blank. Not a single button, lever or switch in sight. "How do you make this thing stop? How do we go back?"

"No back. Only forward," the mole with the clipboard sighs.

The elevator dings and the doors open as I land with a horrendous smack in the middle of the burial mound.

Chapter Fourteen

Fields shimmer along the edge of the burial mound. It's the creepiest place in the world. Bones stick up through the dirt. I roll away making a *bleh* sound that mirrors how I feel. I know this isn't a dream because dreams rarely have this much dirt. Tangled in the strap of my messenger bag, I stand and stumble to the ground. The whole mound is sectioned off with plastic tape and *keep out* signs. So much for the *keep out* part, I think, dusting off my hoodie.

I must get back to the farmhouse. I run full speed and pound up the stairs. Rounding the corner, I stop in the doorway. Bright sunlight floods my bedroom, so bright it makes me squeeze my eyes shut. Opening my eyes, I see my suitcase untouched on the dresser. Everything is exactly where I left it. No Assassin Bug on the rug. No moles with aviator goggles and spears. No signs of life at all except for the faint smell of biscuits. Walking across the rug, flecks of dirt fly down to the floor. Rich, dark earth from tunnels that lead down to boats. Tiny, dry reminders.

At that moment I know it isn't a dream. There's no way I just ended up at that creepy mound without the rest of the journey being true. There must be proof. Tiny footprints or aviator goggles on the hardwood floor. Stumbling from one corner to the next, I see everything exactly as before. Catching sight of my reflection in the antique mirror my blue hair glows in the light. A wild twinkle in my eye catches my attention. A spark. The dull ache of leaving home is gone. Maybe I like that part. Maybe I like floating on the surface of time because let's be honest, back in B-more I was mostly killing time.

I drop to my knees and look under the bed. It's so high off the floor I can slide under. Dust, old boxes. No Assassin Bug. Just sunlight pulsing on the hardwood floor.

Rowan calls up the stairs. "Maya Loop?"

Stalling for time I don't answer. Think back. Rowan, the killing jar, the lights in the fields, and the moles...

The hole!

Pushing the dresser away from the wall, I hunker down to have a look. A breath catches in my throat. If it isn't real, then how could I have known about the mouse hole? In a wild blur, I adjust my messenger. I'm going on an adventure of dangerous peril. I just know it. This is the shiznizzle.

The sound of footsteps on the stairs makes me freeze. I stay on the floor, peeking around the corner of the dresser. Rowan will either be cool with the bug situation or not. I haven't been out in the sticks long enough to accurately predict. I'm guessing not. *Not* fills me with *ugh*. *Not* is my least favorite word. *Ugh* is dread with drama attached.

Somewhere there is an elevator in the middle of a meadow and I have to find it to find the Assassin Bug before the Landions make humans disappear forever.

"Maya?" Rowan calls from the upstairs hall.

I push deeper into the spot between the dresser and the corner.

A second later his footsteps stop in my room. He clears his throat. "I can see your green combat boot sticking out. I know you're in here."

Peeking around the corner I see he looks totally irked.

"What have you done?" he hisses.

"I wasn't going to let him die," I say, adjusting my strap as I push myself upright.

"It wasn't your choice."

I can hold my own in a stand-off. Playgrounds in Baltimore are notorious for making people put up or shut up. "When a life is on the line, it kinda is my choice."

"My dad is furious. He thinks I did it."

"So, tell him it got loose."

"First of all, I'm not lying to my dad. Second of all, you put the lid back on the jar, and didn't even try to make it look like an accident."

Technically, he's right. Holding him in my best girl power glare, I shift my bag. "Okay, I'm sorry about that. I've binge-watched enough crime scene shows to know I should have left the lid unscrewed and wiped my fingerprints."

"Well, at least you can admit you were wrong."

"About the crime scene, yes. About the bug, no."

"You're really annoying."

"So are you."

Rowan stares at my messenger bag. "Where are you going?"

"I lost something." Which is kinda true, if kinda true is really vague. If a bug is captured by the enemy then, technically, he is lost. I am going to do this thing. I will find that Assassin Bug.

"What could you have possibly lost?"

This is where I gamble. After a nice long pause, I say, "That bug."

His eyes go wide as his mouth drops open. "You *stole* it and then *lost* it?"

Pushing past him, I snort. "You're such a drama queen."

"Then we have to find it," he says. "We can put it back."

Total agreement. Totally different reasons. I'm not putting that bug back in the Killing Jar. He's going to roam free like every other Assassin Bug.

In the kitchen I find a covered plate next to a note. Lifting the edge of the aluminum foil, I smell warm biscuits. Not a lot of biscuits back in B-more. I lived off spicy pork steamed buns at Fong's Kitchen. Biscuits have their place. Plus, they can be crammed in a messenger bag. Plus, he left me a small jar of homemade pickles with my name on the label. Granddaddy is a pickling freak. I stuff the pickles in my bag.

The note reads:

Ground Rules

One.

Home at dark. Period.

No exceptions.

Two.

Where there's fields, there's mice.

Where there's mice, there's snakes.

Wear your boots.

I look past the faded knees on my jeans, to my glitter green combat boots, and smile. Following the rules is easy peasy. The old rusted gear sits on the porcelain sink. It's heavy, but I grab it because I can use it to knock someone out. I stuff it in my bag with my breakfast. Weapons might come in handy since things have gotten weird.

I have only one question for the country boy next door.

I turn around to find him standing in the doorway, frowning.

"Are you going to help me find that bug or not?" I ask.

A big, glowing, orange sherbet sun hovers in the east. I start down the wooden steps into the yard. Behind me, the screen door slams shut.

Rowan yells, "You got me in trouble, and you're just going to walk off?"

Blue-haired girls from Baltimore are pressed for time and boys are a monster pain.

Glancing left, then right, to see if any of the farmhands are hanging around, I say, "Look, I've already gotten myself into big trouble, and you can help me, or not help me, but I have to go."

"What are you talking about?"

I lean forward, whispering urgently. "That Assassin Bug I set free was waiting on me when I got home. He took me to this strange world, where he was kidnapped. I'm pretty sure if I don't get him back, it'll be the end of humans."

Rowan blinks. "Is this why you got sent out here? Because you're crazy?"

Boys calling me crazy isn't new. Boys are the original haters.

"Probably." I shrug.

"How do you know it will be the end of humans?"

"Because he told me."

He stares right at me, speaking slowly. "A bug told you?"

I nod, but my eyes scan the fields, looking for the moles.

"How did the bug tell you?"

"He talked to me. He was waiting upstairs. I already told you."

Rowan's mouth drops open. "What have you done?"

"What have I done?" I cock my head to the side, all sassy like Totsie does. "I didn't do anything."

He frowns. "Well, not—" he huffs. "Look, I've seen things."

"What kind of things?" I ask slowly.

"It wasn't just the lights. There were other things. Not what you're talking about, but yes, I knew something was going on."

"How? How did you know?"

Rowan hesitates, looking away. "There were these shadows over by the burial mounds. Strange and huge. And I've been dreaming about this small bird. It's such a weird dream."

The wind is perfectly still, amplifying the chills running up and down my arms. "A dream of a blind sparrow?"

Rowan's eyes shoot down at me, "How did you know that?"

"Because I had the same dream."

Now we are silent. Two people standing in the middle of forever. One waits for the other to move or breathe or alter the moment.

I don't know what to say, so I say the only thing that makes sense. "I have to go."

"How are you going to find him?"

"I draw a door," I say.

Rowan's got that *you're totally crazy* look again.

Eager to prove him wrong, I flip open my messenger bag. Taking out the sketchpad, I flip to a blank page. "I draw a door," I say, totally serious.

The way I see it, I've got two outcomes. Both will require explaining.

Chapter Fifteen

At the end of the dark tunnel, a lantern glows on the stone floor. Still holding my sketchpad, cool air blows against my cheeks. The deep, rich smell of dirt fills my lungs.

Rowan turns in a complete circle, confused. "Whoa. Where are we?"

I watch him, eyebrow raised. "I don't know exactly. Maybe under the fields. But this is where he brought me before so I know we're on the right track."

"Wait a minute," Rowan says. "The bug brought you here?"

Stuffing the sketchpad into the space next to Mr. Wibbles, I gather all of my courage. "Yes. Come on."

Down the stone path I run, picking up the lantern for darker tunnels up ahead. Doors line the path on either side of the river. Hall after hall of doors so dark and long they look like they go on forever.

"What is going on?" Rowan's voice echoes. It isn't the question that bothers me, it's the tremble in his voice.

My lips twist into a frown. "I can't explain it, but this is exactly how it happened before. If I can get back to the meadow then I can find the Assassin Bug."

Rowan yells, "So, how do we do that?"

"Shhhh," I say, worried he will draw attention to us. "It's a weird riddle. You have to go down to go up."

"That's impossible."

"So is drawing a door and then walking through it to a completely different place."

Catching up to me finally, he says, "Okay, good point."

Together, we round the corner and a hallway of doors lines both sides.

A few doors are wooden, some metal, some so old they peel and crumble into piles of dust. So old they will never open again. That worries me. What good is a door that no longer opens?

"What are we looking for?"

My eyes sweep across the rocky ceiling. Shadows hover our heads. "A bell. I think there is a bell somewhere, and I have to be the one to ring it."

Suddenly, a small voice says, "History repeats itself."

We spin toward the sound and see a mole with bright blue armor and a tiny little helmet.

"That mole is talking," Rowan says, wagging his finger in that direction.

The mole looks Rowan in the eyes. "Yes, upright boy. Your kind aren't the only ones with a gift for words. Words are a collection of thoughts, and thoughts are just like lightning. Anyone can have thoughts."

"Listen," I say, urgently. "I need to help someone I met last night. An Assassin Bug. Have you seen him?"

"He's in the room full of danger."

"Okay, how do we find it?"

The mole points down the tunnel. "That way," he says.

"But …" I insist. "I don't know my way around, and this is already confusing. Can you just take us there? I'm afraid to go too far from home."

"You're already far from home," the mole says, matter-of-factly.

Rowan and I look at each other, knowing it's true.

"Okay." Fear rises in my throat. This is a long way to go for a bug I've just met. "So where do we go?"

"Follow the path."

"That's not much to go on," I say, a little annoyed.

"Never is."

"It seems like I'm going to waste a lot of time trying to find my way."

"Then just remember that *now is now is now*."

Rowan grabs my hand and pulls me toward the stone path. "He's just going to keep talking in riddles," he huffs. "We'll find our way."

"But I…" I blurt out. There is very little time even if *now is now*. "Thank you," I yell to the mole.

"A great challenge awaits you. The upright boy will only slow you down."

"But he's ahead of me," I point out.

"Not for long," the mole says.

Opening my mouth to protest, I am stopped by the sensation of wind on my cheeks. I turn quickly and see Rowan opening a door.

"No!" I lunge forward, too late.

Chapter Sixteen

Landing face first in the grass knocks the breath out of me. Gasping for air, I roll over and see a deep green forest. For as far as my eyes can see there are lush, thick leaves. Flowers perfume the air. Rowan rolls over onto his back, coughing.

Forcing myself to my feet I demand, "What have you done?"

"Me?" he says indignantly. "You're the one with the talking bugs and riddles and doors."

"We're not supposed to open those doors."

"Then why did you draw them?"

"I didn't draw those doors," I say, frustrated. "They were already there the last time. Now you've done it." Putting my hands on my hips, I look around for a way out.

"Well, then where are we?"

"Stand up," I say. "We have to figure out how to get back to the tunnel."

"Can't you just draw a door?"

Flipping my bag open, I pull out my sketchpad. A loud rumble gets my attention. "We're not alone," I whisper, backing into a set of leafy bushes.

The rumbling makes the leaves tremble. Suddenly, a strange little car skids to a stop. A cross between a scooter and a convertible for a small child, with gears and knobs and an open back.

A strange little creature in the strange little car yells over the loud engine. "Long way from home, are you?"

"I don't even know where home is," I say truthfully.

Small, barely a foot tall, he's all soft and wobbly looking with long whiskers and pointy little ears that twitch.

"If it's all the same to you, maybe you could show us the way back home," Rowan says.

I step forward. "Wait. I was going to talk to the Orb Weaver but I couldn't get in, and then my friend was kidnapped—"

"He's not your friend," Rowan snaps, "He's a bug."

"Excuse me," I say quickly, "but you don't know that. And besides, he's in trouble. And I like to think that if I were in trouble someone would help me."

The strange little creature cuts the engine. A last hiccuping gasp explodes out of the tailpipe before it sputters into silence.

Finally, the creature sighs. "I can't take you to the Orb Weaver, but I can take you to the River of Great Divide."

"Yes," I say, excited. "That's where the Assassin Bug said I needed to go."

The strange little creature whispers. "They are using him as a trap for the human girl."

"Who is the human girl?"

His eyes dart past my face to Rowan, then back to me. "Why, you're the human girl. The one with the blue hair who comes to save her world."

I shift uncomfortably under the weight of my messenger bag.

"So," the strange little creature says, "my name is Shooptee. And if you climb aboard then I can get you close to the River of Great Divide. From there you may be able to free your friend."

Rowan stares at the weird car. "Umm... we cannot fit in your car. It's barely big enough for one of us."

Shooptee sighs. "Then you follow. You must hurry. They're coming. They're always coming"

Rowan tosses his pack into the back and stands with his feet on either side. I squeeze in next to him, my messenger bag firmly slung over a shoulder.

"Okay," we say in unison, neither one very sure. The engine roars to life, spitting a weird goop out the exhaust, chortling and churning.

Two Landions holding spears step out from behind trees. Shooptee swings wide on the path, plowing through a bush. I wrap my arms around my head and throw myself forward, trying not to fall out of the tiny car. The Landion's feet make a terrible noise striking the earth. Shivers grab hold of my gut and pull hard. My feet and legs fit in the back of the strange little car, but I am much taller. Loud hisses stream through the air. It's the sound of the world closing in. I just know it. I squeeze my eyes shut for a second. At that very moment, the car lurches forward and my arms flail around my head. I hate the feeling of falling even more than the dark. I grab hold of the seat. The strange car speeds forward and I pray some Landion doesn't snatch me up. I am about to open my eyes and let the breath I've been holding out when suddenly Rowan screams. My eyes pop open. Rowan isn't there. Holding on with one hand, I swing around for the briefest moment and watch him hit the ground. Stunned, he tries to stand and run, but the Landions grab his arms and jerk him to his feet

"Rowan!" I scream. "No!"

For a tiny second the car slows, not much, but enough to feel it and I turn back around, yelling to Shooptee. "We have to go back!"

"No back. Only forward," Shooptee yells, stomping on the accelerator, making the car speed faster than before.

The fear in Rowan's eyes makes my whole body tighten. He screams for help, but I can't jump out. Not now. We'll both be captured. No one even knows we are here, so who will save us? I don't even know where we are or how to get back. Holding tight is my only choice. Shooptee grunts, shifting, fiddling with gears and gadgets. Rowan's face pinches in a horrible way as tears fall down his cheeks. The Landions lift him off of the ground.

"Nooo!" Rowan twists and jerks, trying to get free. I'm about to yell that I'll get him, no matter what, but it's not a great idea to tell the Landions my plan. I know deep down in my soul that blue-haired girls from Baltimore don't leave their friends behind. The thought gives me courage as forest leaves swallow up the car and I lose sight of Rowan.

"Keep your eyes open for Landions," Shooptee yells. "They're everywhere."

At a sharp turn around a grove of trees, the strange little car descends down a dirt path that cuts beneath branches so low I must bend down, cheek to cheek with Shooptee. The fur on his face is soft, and smells like jellybeans and lavender.

Chapter Seventeen

"These things set in stone," Shooptee yells over his shoulder, gripping tight to the steering wheel.

"What is?" I yell back over the noise of the engine.

"The boy," he yells. "Saw it. Predicted long time ago. Shooptee know."

"But that can't be," I yell. "We just got here."

Shooptee takes a corner fast. "Not how time works."

The entrance to a tunnel is ahead. My eyes go wide. The tunnel is thick brush hollowed out to conceal it, to make it easy to enter. Except, the tunnel isn't much bigger than the car. I throw my entire body flat, cramped in the tiny space. With my face in the front seat next to Shooptee, we enter the dark tunnel. The scent of rich dirt and old leaves fills the air, rushing past my face.

"Humans see time as illusions. Not really that way. Humans whack whack about time. All wrong. So wrong."

A light clicks on at the front of the car. Twisted branches glow. The car zooms through the tunnel.

"What illusions?" I ask, sneaking peeks this way and that.

"That there is one world," Shooptee grunts, shifting gears, taking a sharp turn. "You think no other world exist so you not work with beings of other worlds. Now Landions going to turn back clock and erase humans. You only one to save your kind. Big job. Humans whack whack,"

"But I can work with other beings. Back in Baltimore, I was a part of the leadership program in school."

Shooptee shakes his head, fur tickling my cheek. "Landions not care."

"But you care. You're helping me."

An amazing burst of light appears at the end of the tunnel. The car careens forward. Amazing sunlight pinches my eyes closed after so much darkness.

"I am special few," Shooptee grunts. "I believe in you. These parts not filled with my kind."

"What will I find?" I ask, grateful to be out of the dark tunnel.

"Landions think, faster get rid of humans, the better."

Even with all the danger and uncertainty, knowing my kind is so disliked makes me sad.

The car jerks to a stop, slamming my forehead into the dash. "Ouch," I try to unfold my body from its cramped position. Rowan's backpack is next to my cheek. It must have fallen to the floorboard.

Shooptee jumps out, running for the front of the car. "Quick and zippy. Help Shooptee."

I push upright, watching. Shooptee pushes a flat wooden cover made from woven vines out of the way. "Zip. Zip. Lazy girl."

I roll out, hitting the ground with a loud thud because it's easier than trying to stand in the small car. Covered in dust and leaves, I lift the cover with one hand and pull it over the hole. Shooptee's eyes are wild with approval. "Humans whack whack but strong."

I frown, pretty sure whack whack means he thinks I'm crazy. Giving the ground one last sweep to check for Landions before letting go of the cover, I look around, but only shadows lead the way. Climbing back into the car, I ask, "Do you live down here?"

"No," Shooptee says, slamming his foot on the pedal. "Live in trees."

I look at the dirt walls as we descend into dark. "The only thing down here is tree roots."

"Not true. This world go down to go up."

The engine of the little car makes an awful grinding noise as it carries us up a treacherous slant. At the top of the dirt tunnel we round a corner, gears straining, into pale light. Then *up, up, up* the little car churns. Cresting the top of the tunnel we roll out onto a wide tree branch.

My eyes go wide as I spin around. "How did you do that?"

Shooptee chortles. "Shoop do many things."

Glancing down, I see the branch is very thick and much bigger than the car. Many branches lead down to a forest floor. Turning around, I have just enough time to duck before the little car rolls onto a landing inside a tree trunk and stops. The smell of wood and flowers fills my nose.

Shooptee pats the big metal steering wheel with his furry hands. "Home," he says. "Time for snacks and finding friends."

The lovely smell of flowers is overwhelming. "What is that smell?"

Shooptee looks me in the eyes. "You smell?"

"Yes," I say excitedly. "It smells amazing."

He stares at me a moment, unable to believe his very furry ears. "That Trulia flower. How we find each other in forest. Trulia like map. Grows on vines in treetops. Shooptee not be spotted up here with flower."

"But doesn't it lead the Landions straight to you?"

Shooptee climbs out of the driver's seat onto the wooden platform. "Landions not smell Trulia flower. Not aware humans can smell either. *Huh.* Until now." His furry face beams.

I throw a leg over the back of the car and test the ledge. "What does that mean?" Tossing Rowan's backpack over one shoulder, my messenger over the other, I step out.

Shooptee puts his hand on a ladder and climbs. "Mean you very special girl."

I adjust the two bags and start to climb, all while contemplating the idea I might be special and what that might mean.

Shooptee grunts and snorts to the top, his hairy butt just above my head. I wonder if being special will help me find Rowan and the Assassin Bug and get home before dinner. The panic of this not happening tightens my throat until my head pops up through the floor. Inside I see a small house in the treetops. The ceiling is so low I must duck, but the view from the windows is magnificent.

"This is where you live?" I ask, breathlessly.

"Shooptee live high," he says, grabbing rolls of paper that look like posters.

"Are you safe up here?"

Shooptee sighs. "Mostly."

"What about the Landions?"

He tilts his head. "Cannot climb. Tethered to ground. That's why they called Landions."

"Because they have to stay on land?"

"Precisely," he snaps his fingers. "But they have dark power. Make life in trees difficult. Their blood is poison. Hearts full of hate."

He rolls open a map, setting jars and bottles on the corners. "Here," he points to a huge red section. "This where Landion camp for now. They travelers. You want to get friends before Landion move again."

"You'll help me, right?"

"Shooptee help you *now*."

"You're going to make me go out and rescue them alone?"

Shooptee's eyes fall to the map. "Much to learn," he sighs.

He pulls a jar from under the table. "I share my favorite Lupa berries. Must get a plan."

"Is there anything you can tell me to make this easier?"

Shooptee pops a small reddish-purple berry in his mouth and chews. "End of world come. No time to plan."

The world ending makes me squirm. "Are there more of you?"

"Shooptee mighty and strong."

The hand-drawn map shows an area with mountains and trees, thick patches of forest and twisty mystic knots like my grandmother collected. A big, thick line runs straight down the middle.

I point. "What's that?"

Shooptee stops chewing. "River of Great Divide." His whiskers pinch up so it suggests he's not sure I can cross.

"The Assassin Bug said I had to cross the River of Great Divide."

"I not go. Shooptee stay here. Eat berry."

I put my hands on my hips. "You're going to send me out there alone?"

Shooptee shrugs. "You have trade?"

"For what?"

"For what Shooptee give you."

I've learned it's best not to agree to trade until I figure out what I'm getting. Playgrounds in Baltimore have their own school lessons. Selfish but true. "What's in it for me?"

He pulls a little basket with a silver dagger out from under the table. I'm thinking a dagger could come in handy.

"Okay." I pull the feather from my pocket and hold its softness in my hand, a moment before laying it gently on the low wooden table.

Shooptee pushes back, looking me up and down.

I swallow, looking around nervously. "I'm sorry. Should I have kept that in my pocket?"

Shooptee opens his mouth and points a hairy finger in my direction. "It is you."

I shrug, self-consciously.

"It is. Word had spread that you would be the one to stop the Landions. *You, a human child.* Humans lost their power years ago."

I hoist my fist in the air. "Girl power!"

Shooptee stares, blinks.

"It's a joke from school. Not very well played. So, what do I have to do?"

"Cross the River of Great Divide."

"You keep saying that."

"Shooptee know it true."

"Do you think that's where they took Rowan and the Assassin Bug?"

"Oh, yes," his furry head nods. "Held in room full of danger." Shooptee points to the map, lowering his voice to a whisper. "Find last piece of ancient clock and hide forever. Landion can never find. Landion find you, you no more exist. Find piece first, Landion not able turn it back."

"Where is the room full of danger?"

97

Shooptee wiggles his whiskers.

"Well?"

"No one come back," he shrugs. "I not know answer."

"What? You're going to send me across a river and you don't even know where I should go?"

Shooptee fumbles with the berry jar, turning back to the map. "That way it is."

"So who was the last human you sent across that river?"

Shooptee stuffs the silver dagger and some tiny spiked balls into my messenger bag.

"Your grandmother."

My stomach sinks way down into my knees. "What?" *That cannot be true.* I am far from home and in danger, as illustrated by the sheathed dagger Shooptee stuffed in my bag. In my current circumstances, I have no reason to believe I will ever get back. She never came back. She's been gone for years and we've all been wondering. A crack inside me breaks open until I can barely breathe. My head falls onto the table with a loud *thunk*.

Shooptee stops stuffing and I feel him staring. "No time sleep. Must go."

Lifting my head only high enough to make eye contact, I say, "But what if I don't return?"

Shooptee wiggles his whiskers. I know he's thinking of a nice way to tell me I'm toast. "Don't succeed, never exist."

I am so annoyed I actually cock my head and huff. Wisps of blue hair tumble down into my eyes. "Well, that doesn't put any pressure on me at all."

Shooptee holds my gaze a second more, then shrugs. "Shooptee never lie."

I look around the room. Finely carved windows in perfect circles and mats woven from thick leaves, low shelves with jars and fat little chairs perfect for a round Shooptee. "So you're saying I have one chance?"

Furrowing his hairy forehead, he sighs, "No human come long time. Landion too much power now." He holds my gaze a second, then blinks and stuffs a small wooden club in the bag.

I put my hands on my hips. "I have to be home in time for dinner or Granddaddy will be worried."

He sighs long and hard, tightening the drawstring on the bag. "Dinner late tonight." Pushing my bag across the table at me, he says, "Now trade."

"We just traded."

"Shooptee give many thing."

"I don't have much in my bag."

Shooptee points at the top of the pickle jar sticking out of my bag.

"You want my pickles?" I don't know how I feel about trading Granddaddy's vinegar treat. On the one hand, pickles are weird. On the other hand, pickles are good. "Okay," I say, finally, "but you better help me, mister."

Shooptee chortles and hides the pickles under the table. His furry butt bobs up and down as he walks to a door that leads out to a branch.

I'm dubious, but I grab my bags and follow.

The second I step through the doorway I realize the maze of walkways and rope bridges is dizzying. Shooptee might be slow on the ground but the speed in which he runs and hops through the branches is impressive. This type of balance would be hard for a well-rested, well-fed, blue-haired girl from Baltimore. Which I am not. The strange berries made me hungrier. I yawn. The lush green leaves are so soft. I can take a nap on a tall branch then ...

"Zip. Zip," Shooptee urges, pulling me onto a rope bridge made of vines.

"Why can't we take your little car thing?"

Squeezing my hand tight, he whispers, "Landion."

I look around nervously, stepping onto the bridge. "Are they here?"

"They're everywhere." His sentence is cut short by a horrific look on his face.

I barely have enough time to say, "Wha—" before I feel the vine bridge give way. My hands grasp desperately at leaves, branches, anything, but—

I am falling down, down, down to the most dangerous place of all. The forest floor.

Shooptee lets out a loud *whomp whomp* noise. Everything is a blur of branches and leaves. Jerking forward, I gasp for breath, looking in every direction for Landions. Up above I hear Shooptee shrieking in the tree. I am waiting for the black eyes and the awful hissing ticking sound. Instead, I fall smack into the middle of the burial mound with a thud that knocks the wind out of my chest.

Again.

A skeletal hand sticks up from the dirt, like a finger poised to turn back time.

Chapter Eighteen

Emergency trucks are parked around the sheriff's car. The sight fills me with a dread so complete I come to a stop on the gravel driveway. It's like my glitter green combat boots suddenly weigh eight hundred pounds. My gut screams *turn back*.

Through the kitchen window, I see the sheriff talking to a man I assume is Rowan's father. My stomach tightens. The same way it did when my mom told me she was going to Afghanistan. I feel like I'm falling inside a tunnel to the center of the earth where I will be swallowed by ticking monsters with black eyes.

Every fiber of my being tells me to run, but I am a complicated blue-haired girl from Baltimore. I have to know. I absolutely have to know if Rowan is in that house. Maybe the emergency vehicles are for some other reason. Maybe he called the cops because I let his bug loose. Reaching, I know, but it could be. I step back and look up at Rowan's window. If I fell back to the creepy mound then he has to be up there with his UFO posters and soft rug.

I'm here, I reason. He has to be here, too.

Ducking through the maze of vehicles I sneak over to the screen door and peek inside. I need to get up the stairs without being seen. That plan is shot down immediately when Rowan's father looks up and sees me. The bug killer says something to the sheriff and they both turn. I back up to run.

"Can I help you?" he asks.

"No," I say and turn to run.

Blue-haired girls from Baltimore know how to run fast.

Behind me, the screen door creaks open. "Are you the girl? Are you Gene's granddaughter?"

I turn and shrug, because maybe I'm the girl, maybe I'm not.

"Rowan—" his father blurts out. "Have you seen Rowan?"

Before I can run, the bug killer is across the driveway, towering over me. The whole scene freaks me out.

I shake my head. "I thought he might be here. That's why I walked over."

"He hasn't been home all day. No note. No nothing. He just set a specimen free and then vanished. I can't even find his footprints out in the yard."

Specimen. That word really bothers me. Also, he didn't vanish. He was taken prisoner. Something tells me if I admit the truth, I'll be here all day explaining that I'm not a total lunatic. Plus, trying to explain the talking bug is a wee bit looney if I do say so myself. I feel certain my time can be better spent. Time to play a riveting game of Dodge the Adults. The man demanding I tell the truth is the same one who tried to kill the Assassin Bug, which would have gotten all humans erased. So, totally not helpful in my opinion.

Another man in uniform walks down the steps, and I use it as an excuse to get away.

"Wait—" the bug killer yells. *Wait* is not my vocabulary word of the moment. I do not wait.

My boots hit the gravel, and I yell, "I'll see if I can find him," which is the truth. Just not the way everyone thinks.

A safe distance away I stop and turn. I expect to see Rowan standing in his bedroom window, watching me through scuffed binoculars. The room and window are empty from what I can see. A dark rectangle in that strange place where earth and sky intersect. Emergency vehicles block the back door. If the bug killer is watching, I can't see him. That gives me the creeps.

Standing out in that field, I suddenly remember countless conversations from years ago. Streaks of flashlights on the walls. Vividly, I remember Granddaddy on the back porch, squeezing my mother's hand tight. Words choked in his throat. Emergency vehicles filling up his driveway. For years, everyone assumed my grandmother vanished without a trace. That she walked out with the intention of returning. Now it is happening all over again. The emergency vehicles are everywhere and another person has not returned. Staring at the scene in Rowan's driveway, I wonder if my grandmother knew. She must have known she was going on a journey into a dangerous world to fight a battle she might not win. She had to know.

And if she knew, she would've left a clue.

Chapter Nineteen

For a brief second, I stop and listen. The house is quiet. I sprint up the stairs. Taking a deep breath, I walk across the hall and into my grandparents' bedroom. For the first time, I notice all of my grandmother's things are left untouched, exactly where they were when she left.

Vividly, I remember Granddaddy on the back porch, staring into the fields. The lights of search crews cutting through the night. I remember the weeks leading up. I remember how strange my grandmother sounded on the phone the last time I talked to her. How she was worried and distracted, a quiver in her voice. I remember the blank postcard she sent. My mom said it was obviously a mistake. That Granddaddy grabbed it and mailed it before she had a chance to write a message.

Standing in the doorway, I have a chilling thought. That postcard does have a message. It must have a message.

My messenger bag is filled with all kinds of stuff. It takes me a minute, but finally, I find the card and pull it out. Blank, except for my name and address, and the postmark. No return address, no message. Nothing.

Slowly, I walk to the top of the stairs. I don't know why. It's like I want the answer more than anything, but I'm completely terrified of the truth. I kneel in front of the bookcase, resting one knee on the floor. The encyclopedias are in alphabetical order. I start at the end and make my way back down the shelf. From Z to V to T. But my eyes stop on S. Very discreetly, my grandmother has written the postmark from the postcard on the spine of the encyclopedia. I open S and see the inside of the large book has been carved out to form a box. It's not a book at all. It's a secret hiding place. There is a picture of a scroll cut from another page. There is a piece of paper with symbols, folded up, old mystic knots.

There is a penny taped to a page, with a note underneath that reads:

Take this. You'll need it if you want to live.

The bottom of the page is torn off.

I shift my weight, but fall into a sitting position on the rug, half-cocked and uncomfortable. I know I should be drawing a door right now, but all I can think about is that my grandmother might really be alive out there, somewhere. The word *alive* surges through the air, electric. It's going to be my job to get her back. In Baltimore, I'm the one who's most likely to take a dare, a double dare, or even the notorious triple-dog-dare.

Page after page of doors drawn in ink. Pages ripped from other books. Some are crossed out, and say, "Do Not Enter," all in caps. There is a map of the fields, and what looks to be the river underneath. In every one there is an X over the burial mound.

I hold the pieces of paper in one hand, stunned.

She knew.

And now I know.

I know deep in my gut she's alive. Glancing at last glowing rays of sunlight streaming over the fields, I might have enough time to get back before dark. I hear the door open downstairs, and I shove the maps inside my bag. I keep the penny out because I want to live.

Granddaddy runs up the staircase and nearly scares me to death.

He steps back, startled, out of breath. "Where have you been? I've been looking everywhere for you."

There is no way to explain where I've been. I jerk my head to the side and glance out the window. The sun blazes up from the horizon like the world is on fire. The thought of no one witnessing a sunset makes me ache.

"I was—" I start, but have no idea what to say. "I was here," I say finally.

"I thought I looked in your room." Confusion pinches the corner of his eyes.

"I was right down the hall." *Because that's true, right?* I was down a hall. Maybe not this one but it was a hall. Because here's my thinking. Maybe I'm crazy or dreaming. Underground tunnels and doors to other timelines and talking bugs might not be real. Maybe I have been sitting here all along, on the floor, daydreaming.

Extending his hand, he pulls me to my feet. "What are you doing on the floor?"

The weight of two bags threatens to pull me back down. "I was just looking through some old encyclopedias."

Granddaddy pulls me in fast for a hug. A big, long, squeezy bear hug. The kind I like. The sudden sensation of being wrapped in his arms makes me feel safe and warm. For a split second, I close my eyes long enough to take a breath.

"I was so worried," he whispers. "I've been looking everywhere. Maybe I was in such a panic that I just didn't see you in your room."

He squeezes me so tight and makes me feel so loved that my forehead falls onto his soft flannel shirt. I breathe in the scent of hay and diesel. I squeeze him super tight. Tighter than I've ever squeezed.

When he finally releases his grip, he sighs heavily, with relief. "Wash up and come downstairs. We're gonna eat soon. I'm going to grab takeout from the Dirty Spoon."

My eyes shift to the windows. Outside the sun is setting. A world dimmed before being extinguished. I don't know if I have time for dinner. I look up into Granddaddy's eyes and realize, for the first time in my life, I've really scared him. It makes my heart hurt.

I'm about to tell him not to worry, because I am going out there to save us all, but that makes me sound crazy.

Granddaddy wipes his hands on his jeans. "Where is the boy?"

Every lie chips my soul, but this one can't be avoided. "We were playing, but then he said he was going home for lunch."

"Did he go towards the road?"

I shake my head.

"How long ago?"

I shrug. "I don't know. A few hours."

He exhales, long and low, eyes drifting up to the white ceiling for answers that won't come, because I have the real answers, the hard to explain answers. I'm the only one with a chance of getting Rowan back.

"Okay, well, we've got everyone out here looking for him. Stay inside. I'll be back soon."

I watch him walk back down the stairs and can barely see the truck in the driveway.

Flipping the sketchbook open to a blank page, I grab my pen to draw a door. I think about the details of a door. The lines, the corners, how it forms on a page, but all I can see in my mind is the look in Granddaddy's eyes just now. In all the years, I've never noticed the sadness. I've never noticed how it stands guard in his green eyes, waiting. Waiting for some new disaster. Waiting for someone he loves to vanish without a trace.

Chapter Twenty

The phone rings in the hall downstairs and almost scares me to death.

"Hello," I say breathlessly, dropping my bag and Rowan's backpack on the hardwood floor.

"What are you doing?" Totsie asks.

I don't know who I expected on the other end of the line, but the sound of her voice is shocking and confusing. "What do you mean?"

"I thought you were on your way here," she says.

"I was," I say.

"*Was?*"

"I mean, I am. I just got a little sidetracked."

"With what? What could be more important than getting back home?"

I don't know who I can tell, but I've got to tell someone, so I whisper, "I think my grandmother is alive and maybe being held prisoner." It sounds totally nuts when I say it out loud, but I don't care.

For a few seconds, the only sound is an echo of breath filling the distance.

Finally, she asks, "Are you sure? How?"

"Well, I'm not sure."

"Then how do you know?"

"There was this Assassin Bug, and he told me."

"Told you what?"

"That she's alive, which I wasn't sure I should believe, but then I found all this stuff she hid in an encyclopedia upstairs."

"The bug told you?"

"An Assassin Bug. Yes."

Totsie pauses longer than I expect, then finally asks, "*Are you okay?*"

The question is a little annoying. I get talking bugs aren't normal, but humans being erased isn't the standard, everyday crisis either. Or drawing doors, or a list of things I don't have time to explain. I admit it's strange, but strange is the new normal.

"Look, I'll tell you everything soon," I say, "but I've got to go."

"You're already too busy to talk to me?"

"It's not like that."

I just sit there, holding the phone.

"It is," she says, and the line goes dead.

I expect an old cockroach with a strange accent to pop out of a mousehole and start talking. Nothing happens. Getting back to a place I never knew existed is my number one priority. I hang up the phone and grab the two bags at my feet.

I am about to step out on the porch when Rowan's dad looks over from the driveway. I suddenly realize he cannot see the backpack. I shift it over my shoulder, but he's already locked eyes on it.

Walking swiftly across the driveway, he points. "Where did you get that?"

Granddaddy spins around in a circle but stops when he sees him reach for the backpack.

I back away. "He left it in my room." But, before I can make up any more lies, he jerks the pack off of my shoulder.

"Wait," Granddaddy says, setting bags of food back on the seat in his truck.

Rowan's dad unzips the top, undoing my careful organization.

Pulling out the dagger, he holds it in his hand, glaring. "What is this? What exactly were you doing when my son disappeared?"

I want to yell I wasn't doing anything wrong, but Granddaddy is watching. Instead of being caught up in drama, I try to focus. I want that backpack. *I need that backpack.*

Granddaddy steps between the two of us, laying his hand on Tom's shoulder. "We'll find your boy," he says, calmly.

Tom stops, his shoulders falling forward. "I'm sorry. I'm worried out of my mind."

The Dirty Spoon is known for its fried chicken and mashed potatoes with gravy. I can smell it from the front seat. Any other day I'd pile a huge plate with extra gravy on the side. But right now, I want that backpack and that's all I want. My eyes follow Rowan's dad across the driveway as he walks back to his car. Beyond him, at the edge of the world a dark, moonless night is hiding, waiting.

I wipe my sweaty palms on my jeans, and say, "I have to use the bathroom."

Chapter Twenty-One

I lock the bathroom door and pull out my sketchbook. I'm about to flip it open to a new page when someone clears their throat. I close the sketchbook fast and hold it tight. Turning around, I see a mole with aviator goggles standing in the corner.

"Hello," he says, politely.

"Where did you come from?"

Staring at me like I'm a complete imbecile, he says, "A series of underground tunnels."

"Listen," I say, leaning in close, whispering, "you have to help me. I've got to get back to—well, I don't know exactly. I think I need to ring a bell, or find the Orb Weaver, or Cross the River of Great Divide. It's hard to tell what I'm supposed to do at this point. Whatever I do dumps me back on the burial mound repeatedly. I feel like I need to be making progress."

"Yes. Loops are very good at leaping."

"Okay, well you need to tell this Loop how to get back to Shooptee, because he's the only one who's been helpful, and even he is strange."

The mole shrugs. "I am not supposed to help you."

I refuse to look away in disgust and lock him in my glare instead. "And yet, here you are."

When he says nothing, I ask, "What's your name?"

"Montford."

"Well, Montford, I'd love to stand around in the bathroom talking to a mole, but I need help. Real help. Not fair weathered moles who show up because they're feeling guilty."

Montford pinches his soft fur into a scowl. Silence falls between us. I honestly don't know what to say.

Montford steps back and gives a funny little bow. "I want you to trust me."

Blue-haired girls from Baltimore do not trust easily. I have an entire list of life rules in my head that literally tell me to trust no one. "Why should I trust you?"

"Moles are forbidden to help humans. As keepers of the tunnels, we must remain impartial, fair. But there is nothing in the rules that says you cannot trust me."

It takes me a minute, but I begin to get his drift. "So, how exactly do I trust you?"

Montford points at the door. I look over, but a plastic air freshener plugged into the outlet gets my attention. A dried-up freshener with the faintest scent of lilac and violets. A reminder of days long gone. The light dims. My breath catches in my throat. Something old and dark threatens to steal me away in all of this silence. Shadows are out there. I can feel them.

"You hold a great secret, Maya Loop."

115

I suck in a long, frustrated breath. Light shimmers on the floor. Like a hurricane hitting shore, I realize that if I can't find the Assassin Bug and my grandmother and Rowan, then everything built by humans disappears. Including this silly plug-in air freshener I've never given a single thought to before now. A world with green rolling fields and flowing streams will arise, but there won't be a single pair of hands to catch an apple falling from a tree. No jazz albums Granddaddy listens to after dinner. Never again will he have to refuse to update to Mp3s or CDs. No songs or roads or towers to the sky. No philosophers asking, "Why?" Just a ripe, empty planet controlled by Landions.

They will argue this isn't a bad thing. Humans aren't perfect. We can do better. I know in my heart we deserve a chance. My grandmother, Rowan, the Assassin Bug, me. I deserve a chance to make this world a better place. Yes, sir. *This girl.* This blue-haired girl from Baltimore deserves a chance.

My footsteps echo across the bathroom tile.

"These worlds are just projections. The Landions are master manipulators of time, but so are you. They can do the same."

I turn and memorize the angle of light spilling across the floor. Montford backs into the shadows.

"Tell me what to do," I whisper.

Montford points at my bag. I pull my sketchpad out to draw a door. Before I finish the final line, I glance over at him. Poised at the infinite edge of a line about to meet another line I hover. I just

116

have to get this right once. One time is all it takes. I squeeze my eyes shut for a brief second, then draw a line that feels like fate.

Chapter Twenty-Two

Old green carpet runs down a narrow hall. No windows on either side, just two doors—one on either end. I feel certain I came through the door behind me, but this is all so new and confusing I can't be sure. The smell of pan-fried dumplings, shrimp with lobster sauce, fried bananas with honey gets my attention. I know exactly where I am.

Fong's Kitchen.

Sweat beads up on my top lip. I don't know how I feel about drawing a door that leads to my favorite kitchen. I don't move an inch. I just stand there, listening to the complete silence. The silence is very suspicious. Maybe drawing doors requires more experience. I didn't return to the underground river. That bothers me a little. Maybe I did it wrong.

Also, Fong's is never quiet.

It is a constant jangle of Fong yelling to the kitchen staff in Cantonese. I know because he was nice enough to teach me a few words.

The narrow hall blocks my view into the kitchen. Steam drifts from a pot. Getting trapped worries me. If everyone is waiting for me to find them, and no one knows where I am, then I don't even want to think about what happens if the Landions get their hands on me.

Fong would never let Landions into his kitchen. Unless they tricked him by placing an order. He doesn't mess around with orders. Fresh and fast, he always yells, holding the handle of a steel wok with a dish towel.

The scent of steamed buns is mesmerizing. Like a rope, it pulls me towards the warm kitchen. I walk carefully down the hall, my stomach growling. From where I am standing I can see Fong, his back to me, stirring a pot.

Just as I'm about to cross the threshold, a voice behind me says, "That's a trick."

Glitter green combat boot in mid-step, I stop, startled. "What?"

"That way leads you astray," I hear Montford say.

I turn in a circle.

"Down here."

I look down to a hole in the baseboard. "Where does it lead?"

"I mean, that's not a real door. It's a trick door and it leads to the room full of danger."

"Everything is a riddle with you."

Straightening his funny little goggles on his forehead, he says, "I am a highly sophisticated insectivore, I'll have you know."

"I thought you weren't supposed to help me?" I ask, suspiciously.

119

"I'm not," Montford shrugs. "I'm just wondering how far you'll go."

"Maybe I'll go farther than any human has ever gone."

His whiskers pinch up and his nose wiggles. "Maybe."

"So, you just showed up to doubt me?"

"Maybe I placed a bet or two."

"You're gambling while I'm trying to get my friends back?"

"I'm here to offer a tip."

Montford turns, pointing to the door at the end of the hall. "The doorway you're looking for is that way."

I glance back at the kitchen. "Then why is this door here?"

"They're trying to lead you astray. If anyone asks, I was never here. Put the penny in your pocket. You are near." He scurries off through the mousehole in the baseboard before I have time to ask my next question.

"Hey," I call out, but protesting is pointless when moles are involved. I've learned as much. If anything could lead me astray at this point, it would be a pan-fried dumpling. A warm, yummy dumpling on a bed of shredded lettuce with the ginger dipping sauce on the side.

Before I overthink the possibility of making the ultimate wrong turn, I push open the door at the end of the hall behind me. A set of stone steps leads down into the dark. There is no part of me that wants to descend into a dark hole. Glancing back towards the kitchen, I inhale deep, but the smell is gone. A loud hissing starts up in the kitchen, and I adjust my messenger bag and run down the stairs. I want to ball my fists tight and clobber whatever comes at me, but I keep my palms flat and feel along the walls. Behind me, the door stays closed, but relief is a luxury I don't have at the moment.

Suddenly, I wish I had a hammer or a sword; wish I'd played more Super Mario or Fortnite with Totsie, and then I'd know how to advance. Secretly, I hope for a pot of gold at the bottom of the stairs, though it won't help me find my friends. All my life I've wasted my wishes on things I don't need. Now all I need is a flashlight, and I don't have one. The stairs go on and on. I listen for sounds of the river.

I am surrounded by pitch black. A dark so complete it feels like I can touch it. A dark so disorienting that standing still makes me feel like I am falling. Leaning my back against the wall, I descend the stone staircase, wide and flat, curving down into twists and turns.

I think about the dream of the sparrow and the flashlight. An overwhelming sense of *déjà vu* takes hold. I wind down, curving this way and that until a warm buttery light spills across the stones.

Chapter Twenty-Three

Stepping around the final corner into a stone room with wooden shelves and a big, golden table in the middle, I see shelves stacked floor to ceiling with jars and tins. Small and cute, the whole room smells like cinnamon sticks.

Behind me, a woman says, "Turn around."

I spin around so fast my messenger bag throws me off-balance. I stumble into a small woman with delicate hands, barely as tall as me.

"I'm sorry," I say, not sure if I should run. Situations of uncertainty are my new normal. "I am looking for this–" I hesitate, thinking about my answer. *What is Shooptee, exactly?* I've never seen anything like a Shooptee in my life. "I, well, there is a Shooptee who wants to show me the way. Can you help me get back to him?"

The small woman touches my hand. "We must hurry."

My eyes trail around the room. It's perfectly round and painted a dazzling blue. "So, you know how to get me back to him? At least, I think it was a boy Shooptee. It's hard to tell."

"Yes," the small woman says. "I will try to get you to the River of Great Divide." She walks quickly to the shelves, her eyes scanning each bottle. One after the other, she sets bottles on the table.

"Do you think I can pull this off?"

The small woman stops and turns to face me, holding something wrapped in brown cloth. "No one has ever returned from the other side of the river."

My fists tighten at my sides the way they do when a teacher announces a pop test. "So, will I make it back?"

The small woman shrugs. "Uncharted territory. I'll do everything I can to make that possible." Lifting a bottle from the shelf, she says, "We'll start by filling your bag. First up is honeysuckle juice."

The thought of sweet juice makes my mouth water. I reach for the bottle, but she pulls away. "Have you ever had honeysuckle juice before?"

I shake my head. "No, but it sounds delicious."

The woman grabs a stack of yellowed paper and shoves it across the table. "You'll want to understand the properties first."

I nod my head, proud of all the good grades that fill up my report card. I can remember facts and number sequences like crazy.

"It must be fresh. I'm giving you the whole bottle. It takes three minutes to take effect."

"Okay. What does it do?"

She unzips the top of the backpack and sets the bottles inside. "If you drink a whole bottle, it will make you invisible. I only have three. You'll have to make do with that."

I am only guessing, but if it really works, then one bottle is pretty cool. I'm not saying I believe this hocus pocus, woo-woo invisibility business. I'm just saying, given the danger I've already encountered, maybe a little honeysuckle juice will come in handy.

"Excuse me," I say abruptly. "I don't mean to be rude, but who are you?"

She dumps a handful of dried flower petals into a bowl and breaks them apart with her hands. "I am Sayrah. I am here to help you with your passage."

"But how did you know I'd come here?"

Sayrah stops crumbling. The flower petals stick to her thumb. "We have been waiting for you since before your grandmother decided to cross."

I back up suspiciously. "What's her name?"

"Sara Louise."

"How could you know that?"

"Because time is different in this world. Different in all worlds really."

I glance around the room nervously, suddenly realizing there are no clocks or windows. Nothing to indicate the passage of time. Also, the only way out is the way I came in, and a small wooden door set in stone next to the shelves.

"I don't understand."

"In your world, humans think time moves forward. That's because of the way you are made. Time is really happening all at once. Backward and forward. Humans just can't see it. It's a terrible design flaw," she sighs.

I furrow my brow. "So, you've seen the future?"

"There is no future here. Or past. Only possibilities. Time is now, is now, is now."

"I've heard that before."

"You'll hear it again."

"Then why do humans even need time if everyone else doesn't?"

Sayrah bends down and pulls a small pouch from under the table. Inside, she stuffs glowing fiery arrows and a small bow and arrow. "Time is control. For us time is alive, flowing. For you, it's a cage. Time locks all matter into that cage and creates suffering. Your world has been suffering a long time."

I adjust my messenger bag. "Well, I'm going to try and get across the river."

Pulling a tight smile, Sayrah inhales sharply. "Not all worlds are filled with kindness. There are dark worlds where goodness is crushed. Worlds where only suffering exists. Stay away from the doors that lead to those worlds." Sayrah pinches powders from bottles and bowls, sprinkling them into pouches. "You are a fierce child. There are many who believe you can do this."

"Do you believe I can do this?"

Stepping close to me, Sayrah stuffs several pouches in my bag. "Everyone believes you can do this. Especially the Landions."

I look down at the pouches and see a tiny butter splotch on my sleeve from dinner last night. Dinner seems so long ago. Like years have passed. Like I was a completely different person. "Okay," I inhale deeply, "what's in all these pouches?"

Pulling a brown pouch out, letting it rest in the palm of her hand, she says, "This is a medicine pouch. If you get lost, take a pinch of powder and put it on the tip of your nose. It will act as a guide." The fiery arrows glow hot at the tip.

"Are those on fire?" I ask, worried about putting anything on fire in my messenger bag.

Sayrah smiles. "They only ignite when they strike their target."

"Yowza. I don't know how to shoot a bow and arrow."

"Ever thrown a rock?"

"From the piers of Baltimore."

"Same principle. Identify the danger. Aim. Make it count. Simple." She gestures around her cute room. "Obviously, we can't practice in here. The most important part is to make it count."

With a certain urgency, she buckles the flaps on my bag and walks quickly to the wooden door. I'm thinking how glad I am that I need not go back up those steps. "Where does this door go?"

"It is my job to prepare you for this part of the journey."

I gulp back my urge to run back to Baltimore and hide under my blanket. I could watch hilarious cat videos all day. I can give up and watch the world end.

Terrible choice.

Moving on.

Sayrah pulls a bottle with a dropper from the nearest shelf. "Open your mouth."

My jaw drops open before I even have time to think about what I'm doing.

"Stick out your tongue."

Sayrah drops three perfect, sweet drops into my mouth.

"That gives you eight hours of power back and forth through time to start over if you need to. After that, you're on your own."

I swallow and nod. "What does that mean?"

"It means you won't bounce around as much, but humans are strange, so it will still be bumpy."

"Bumpy?"

"Do you have your penny?"

"Yes."

"Take it out and hold it tight in your hand."

I fumble through my pocket as she jerks open the wooden door. I can see nothing on the other side.

When I have my penny in hand, Sayrah says, "I can prepare you, but you have to go alone. I have kept you too long because I like you. Your grandmother is a hero. You must take these things and use them to cross the River of Great Divide, or convince the Orb Weaver to weave you into a timeline. Beyond that, all I can offer is fiery arrows and faith, for no one has ever crossed that river and returned."

Then, she pushes me over the threshold.

Chapter Twenty-Four

I come face to face with the biggest snake I've ever seen. I spin back around and see the closed door. I slowly turn around. Bowls of pennies fill the room behind the snake's enormous black and golden head. Cooper pennies shine golden in the light of a few candles melting onto the stone floor. Piles of bones in each corner make me shiver.

"What is thissssssssss," the serpent hisses.

I back into the door, jiggling the knob, but it won't open. I don't even know what to say. How do I introduce myself to a giant snake? Clutching my messenger bag, I manage a forced smile, tight and fake, but it's all I've got.

"A girl child." The serpent slithers in a circle, rising up in front of me. Sliding her head over my bag she asks, "What have you brought, girl child?"

"Things to find my friends who were taken by the Landions. They need my help."

"There are no Landions here. You need *my* help. All humans moving through time must first find a penny that enables you to pass. It says so in the Book of the Moon. Have you read it?"

I shake my head as the serpent coils over my cheeks. I wonder which is scarier, the dark or snakes? Her terrible tongue flicks inches from my nose. Having just experienced both, I can honestly say snakes are scarier.

I stammer, trying to pull my words together. "Well, maybe not here in this room, but near."

"Near?" the serpent repeats. "The only thing here is me, and I have been here a long, long time. Maybe even a million years, if I had to guess, which I don't have to, because guessing is silly."

"That's a long time."

"Do you like to guess, girl child?"

I'm guessing when I shake my head.

"*Hmm...*" she says softly, bobbing her head up and down, which makes her look like she's smiling.

"Why are all these places so unfriendly?"

The serpent's head hovers above the palm of my hand like she's floating in mid-air. "Because humans destroy everything they touch."

"I have never destroyed anything in my life."

"Never smacked and killed a fly for getting on your nerves?"

I cock my head. "Never."

Cocking her head in the opposite direction, she asks, "Never smashed a slug on your way home from school?"

"Never."

"Never killed an entire colony of ants with those awful cans of poison?"

"That's terrible. Ants are sophisticated and intelligent and bury their dead."

Pulling her head back she eyes me up and down. "Never worn a pair of those dreadful snakeskin shoes?"

Proudly, I hoist up a glitter green combat boot for inspection. "I'm strictly vegan glitter."

The serpent exhales quietly. "Perhaps you are the real deal."

The serpent slides up the wall beside me. An image appears, fuzzy at first. Every muscle in my body tightens. It's like a movie with no sound, except it's not make-believe, it's me and my friends back in B-more. Tizzy and Lemon Drop pull open the door of the corner market for Totsie. We bump shoulders, laughing.

I turn to face the serpent so she can see my eyes. "You've been spying on me."

She shakes her black and gold head. "Not spying. At least, not the way you think."

"How are you even doing that?"

Pulling her head from the smooth stone, the image disappears. "Thoughts are simply a projection. Humans use all kinds of devices to transmit ideas and images. That is not necessary for us. We don't need a device. We simply project with our minds. You think of it as memory, but that is incorrect. They are impressions and impressions are imprinted everywhere."

Laying her head back on the stone wall, the image reappears. This time, inside the store. I stand in line with my friends, our arms full of cupcakes and chocolate milk and bags of mini powdered doughnuts. For a fleeting second, a tiny second, I want to go back to the past. Not just back to Baltimore, which is my goal, but back to days long gone. Back to rows of buildings facing that mysterious line where the sun rises up from dark water. Back to games of UNO and Fortnite, making silly videos, sleepovers, eating marshmallows and powdered doughnuts from the bag, epic games of Spot-It and I Spy. A time of crazy, wild laughter before people disappeared, before people died, before people were taken prisoner.

"Can you take me back to the past?"

"I can't take you back, but you can find your way back to rooms that haunt you. If you choose."

I look her directly in the eye, trying to figure out who's side she's on. "Why is this happening?"

The serpent slithers away from the wall, returning to the space right in front of me. The disappearing image sends a cold chill up my arms.

"Humans are in a cycle of chaos and destruction, unlike any the worlds have ever seen. After the Landions battled for possession of Earth and lost because of Handsome Lake, a set of laws was handed down. Humans have not respected these laws. Neither have the Landions. This is a collision course. Those laws are set to expire, and when they do, the Landions only need to reconstruct the World Clock and turn it back."

My one real superpower is going straight to doom, so I ask, "Are you going to kill me?"

The serpent hisses loudly, pulling back. "Who told you such a thing? Is that what they are saying about me now?"

"No. No one said that. Well, I mean, I said it just now."

"Why would you say such a thing? Why does everyone hate snakes?"

"Because you're very big and kinda scary," I gulp.

The serpent uncoils herself and slithers to the center of the room. "You make me weary, girl child. Choose a penny. Choose well, or you'll be dead."

My face pinches tight. "Dead?" Now I know why I need the penny. Still, I hope it's the right one. When death is on the line, I definitely need the right penny. Correct change is important.

"Dead," she repeats, her eyes drifting to the ceiling in contempt, or boredom. Hard to tell. I've never met a snake before. "The only way to save your people is to choose wisely."

"So, if I pick the wrong penny then—" I pull my finger across my throat the way kids do in Baltimore when someone wants to say it's over, without talking in class.

"Yes," she hisses, coiling into a prim circle, her head rising from the center.

Bowls of all shapes are stacked on the floor. Glass bowls, wooden bowls, blue bowls, old bowls, big bowls, small bowls, metal bowls. Each overflowing with shiny copper pennies.

My palm turns damp and clammy. I swallow back my fear. "Was my grandmother here?"

"Yes," the serpent hisses. "Choose your penny, girl child."

Walking quickly to a bowl, I pretend to look. Secretly, I'm hoping giant serpents can't read minds, because if she can, I'm done for. Nervous and sweaty, I stop in front of a purple bowl. Carefully, I hold the penny tight in-between my index finger and thumb while plunging my hand into the bowl. Cool pennies slide past my fingers. A second later, I pull my hand out, open my palm like a magic trick, and reveal one glowing penny. Which is kinda weird, I admit, because it didn't glow like that back in the room. The coin pulses with light.

With excitement, I turn and say, "This one."

"You're sure?"

Well, I was sure before she asked. "Do I get to keep it?"

"If you're sure."

I'm only kinda sure. "I'm sure."

"Hold tight to your penny, girl child, and wave goodbye."

I squeeze the penny and feel its warm light. I'm just about to ask what happens next when the floor beneath me opens up and I drop, falling through a dark pit, screaming.

Up above me, the serpent hisses, "You chose well girl child."

The trap door in the floor closes. I'm falling so fast in the dark it feels like I'm floating.

Maybe I'm hyperventilating. Hypochondria is real, girl, Totsie would say if she were here, which she isn't, and maybe I'm okay with that because the only thing worse than falling into a pit is dragging my best friend down with me. The school nurse once told me I'm terrible about hyperventilating when I'm really upset. One

133

time, some mean kids pushed Totsie down the stairs. I was so upset I couldn't breathe. Pretty sure I can't breathe now. The only difference is that I'm probably falling into the mouth of a giant monster, ready to gobble me up.

A second later I hit the ground with a loud *whack*.

Chapter Twenty-Five

The loud *whomp* rattles me to the bone. The sound of glass clinking makes me think I looped back around to the farm. I groan and crack one eye open. Shooptee holds a purple teacup in one hand, staring at me like I'm from another planet, which I might be. Hard to tell at this point. Aside from that, I have never been so happy to see a strange, furry being in all my life.

Pushing up from the floor, I feel a deep ache in my bones. Something in my messenger bag glows. I flip open the top and stand back. The fiery arrows are particularly bright.

Shooptee exhales loudly. "Tea for two. Give Shooptee time to prepare. Shooptee not know you coming." He furrows his hairy brow and stares. "I see bag on fire. You probably cannot stay."

I poke at the arrow and it dims. It's not hot, so I pull it out and hold it in my hands. A mystic knot carved into the side glows. A perfect, golden glow.

"I was here," I say, "and then there was a woman, and she gave me a bunch of stuff to put in my bag, and then she shoved me through a door and there was this enormous snake—"

Shooptee's eyes widen and he squeezes the teacup with both hands. "*You saw Ursula?*"

"The snake has a name?"

Shooptee makes a little *pffft* sound. "All snakes have name."

Feeling silly, I change the subject. "So, I have honeysuckle juice and fiery arrows, but no one ever seems to be able to help me, and I got dropped back at the farm. Then a mole named Montford showed up, but he just talked in riddles, and you've just got to help me. I'm serious. I have got to get to the River of Great Divide. You are the only one who can help me."

Shooptee blinks. Setting his teacup on the counter, he grabs a knife, smiling. "Take Shooptee's trusty knife."

I reach for his arm. "I'm taking you." He's so soft, softer than a cat.

Staring out from under his hairy eyebrows, he does not look like he's in the mood for adventure. "No Shooptee come back crossing Great Divide."

"You've tried?"

"All Shooptee try."

"How many?"

"All but me. I last Shooptee." He leans forward, whiskers twitching.

A sense of dread fills me head to toe.

Clapping his hands, his furry cheeks jiggle. "You chose wisely and got past Ursula, but now you hurry." The feathery soft fur on his face blows as he inhales and exhales.

The deep silence of his warm kitchen makes me want to sit at the table and eat cookies. I close my eyes to gather my courage, but all I see are shadows in the fields. "Do you have anything to help me get to the Great Divide?"

Shooptee holds a finger in the air. With the other hand, he digs through a jar on the counter. I'm hoping it contains powdered doughnuts or snickerdoodle cookies. After a second, he removes a seed. With his strange little wobble, he walks over and places it in the palm of my hand.

"What is this?"

"Lotus seed."

I look around the quaint little room. Surely, he has a sword or another dagger, being stuck up here in the forest all alone. "That's it? That's all you got? *A seed?*"

Shooptee's whiskers twist into a frown. "Lotus seed powerful."

I huff and stuff the seed into my pocket.

Shooptee points. "Great Divide that way."

I roll my eyes. "Thanks."

When he doesn't move, I say, "You're really going to send me out there by myself? All alone?"

I raise an eyebrow. I need a weapon. A laser beam, hand grenade.

He stares at me, whiskers twitching. "Now, give Shooptee something."

Words tumble through my brain. "I didn't pack anything extra."

Shooptee points at Mr. Wibble's head sticking out of my bag.

"No way," I shake my head. "You already talked me out of my pickles. Wibbles stays with me."

Shooptee's lip pinches up, bunching his whiskers out on the side. "You no trust Shooptee. Give back seed. Bye-bye."

The tone of his voice makes my heart sink. There were many Shooptee at one time. A mighty tribe of Shooptee. If he really is the last one, then maybe I should be nicer and maybe I should let him keep Wibbles. "Okay," I say, pulling Mr. Wibbles from my bag. "This is a loan for the Lotus Seed."

"Loan?"

"You give me Mr. Wibbles back when I return your seed. Got it?"

Shooptee claps his hand excitedly. "Loan. Loan."

Before I have time to think about what I'm doing, I walk out the door, onto the wide branch, and run.

Chapter Twenty-Six

Running through treetops is harder than it sounds. Some branches are wide enough to run on, but my bag shifts and knocks me off-balance. Wind blows through upper branches and smells like rich, perfumed flowers. Candied violets and sugared jasmine. An entire forest full of candied flowers mixed with the smell of water and earth, damp and green. A breath swells in my chest, deep and urgent.

Reaching forward, I feel a weird tingling up my arms. Down below, something moves.

Excited by the possibility of finding another Shooptee, I lay flat against the branch, its scratchy bark against my cheek, and stare down at the exact same spot until my eyes adjust.

I try desperately to swallow back a tiny gasp.

A Landion looks straight up into the tree.

I freeze. My messenger bag feels like it's going to slide over the edge. Precious seconds filled with dread consume me. I need a plan. If my bag falls, I'll climb higher and make a run for it. But, since I lost the backpack, I *really, really* need my messenger bag. I cannot afford to lose it now.

Wait. Honeysuckle juice.

Holding my breath, my eyes sweep across the ground. The dust colored Landions are easily camouflaged on the forest floor. With their strange, military armor and spears, helmet-shaped heads and long, insect-like arms they are scary even from above. Seeing one is enough to make me gasp, but as my eyes adjust I realize, with a bone-chilling terror, there are hundreds on the ground. Directly beneath me. Their black eyes turn up towards the branch, and a horrible hissing and ticking sound fills the forest floor.

Okay. Stay calm. Don't breathe. Make no sound. My heart pounds against the tree limb. One of them lays a palm on the tree trunk. Stricken with horror, I know he can feel my heartbeat. I push up to get inside my messenger bag. One bottle is all I need to become invisible. As I shift, the lotus seed in my pocket rumbles like it's waking up.

The smell of smoke from a campfire wafts through the air. Without warning the lotus seed slips from my pocket, passing branch after branch until it smacks the ground, right in front of a Landion. Before my eyes, the seed bounces twice, and then hundreds of me appear.

Stunned, I try to hold on tight, watching Landions chase hundreds of me.

I'm the real me, right? Yet, from the branch, I watch hundreds of Maya Loops take off running in every direction.

"Go," someone whispers.

My eyes go wide, and I think Shooptee must have changed his mind. I whip my head around to find two small creatures behind me on the branch.

"I'm Spanky," one of them says, "and this is Mr. Wibbles."

It is Wibbles. At least it looks just like him. Except that can't be. Wibbles is a stuffed animal. A stuffed duck in a fox costume.

"Shooptee said you need help," Wibbles says.

"How are you real?" I touch his ears. Round like a blueberry with a long, bushy tail, ears pointed on top of his head, with his duck bill and webbed feet.

"You need to run," Spanky whispers.

Looking down, I see all but one Landion chasing hundreds of me. I adjust my pack quickly and stand. Running across the wide limb, I hop to the next tree. I do not stop. I do not think. This is no time to lose my balance. Only one direction calls.

The River of Great Divide.

A loud chittering sound erupts from the forest floor as the Landions chase hundreds of blue-haired girls in all directions. Up ahead, through the leaves, I catch sight of the river. A space so vast and wide, from up here I have no idea how to cross. Beyond the river is what looks like a vast desert of static.

The Landions will chase me the entire way. *If they don't catch me first.*

Life back home did not prepare me for this. My soft bed did not prepare me. The warm glow of my chat screen in our tiny kitchen did not prepare me.

The chittering below is deafening.

I run to a wide branch extending out over the water. I have no idea what to do.

Spanky yells, "Jump!"

Ummm…no way.

Mr. Wibbles leaps onto my shoulder. "If you don't jump, we'll all die," he yells.

Once upon a time.

A brave girl.

Small for her age.

With blue hair.

Who can swing higher than anyone else on Earth.

Used to lie in bed in Baltimore, light spilling in, and imagine what would happen if she could walk through doorways and erase the past.

That is what I'm thinking right now.

That is what I'm thinking when I jump.

Chapter Twenty-Seven

Landions are lined up as far as my eyes can see. I feel like I'm being swallowed by a black hole. My heart is beating so fast, I'm going to pass out. Dark rises up from the bottom of the river. An arrow pierces the air right in front of my face. I gasp and jerk my head back, and suddenly realize something is breaking my fall. Looking up I see Wibbles and Spanky holding onto a kind of parachute. I'm holding onto their small feet.

I rock forward, trying to use my weight to get us to the other side of the river. Warm, dusty air dries my throat. Beneath me, the river thrashes.

Arrows slice past my arms.

Mr. Wibbles screams.

My head jerks up. "Are you okay?"

"No, I'm not okay. They're shooting at us!"

I push my arms wide. Spanky lets out a gasp as wind catches our widened sail.

My eyes sweep across the water below. The sun sits on the horizon. A glowing orange glare waiting to see if we win or lose this round. Spanky and Mr. Wibbles rock their bodies, trying to control direction.

Night is coming fast. I don't want the dark, but it might be good cover. I don't know how we're supposed to cross this huge expanse of desert, and I seriously hope we don't land in the river.

An arrow whizzes past, grazing my finger. Blood drips down onto the strap of my messenger bag. My finger burns but holds on tight.

Float. Breathe. Dodge arrows.

A wall of static opens beneath us.

A rush of fear fills my voice. "What is that?"

Spanky yells back. "This is beyond our expertise. You need a Reclamation Specialist."

"A what?" In the midst of urgency, I have a split second to figure out a plan. Blue-haired girls from Baltimore are known for their plans.

The static disappears.

"There," yells Spanky.

A man carrying a funny blue bag tossed over his shoulder stands next to a beat-up truck on the vast expanse of dusty plains. The last rays of sunlight make the shock of white hair on his head stand out.

I gulp back a heavy fear rising in my throat.

He cups his hands around his mouth and yells, "You must be the girl."

Behind me, arrows shoot through the sky. I am almost over the truck, flying low enough to let go, then tuck and roll.

"I have to go," I yell to Spanky and Mr. Wibbles. "Head for that static if it pops up again. It makes it hard to find you."

"Wait—" Mr. Wibbles yells.

Too late to wait. I let go and feel the sensation of falling take hold.

"What are you doing?" Spanky screams.

"Saving the world," I yell back, as my glitter green combat boots hit the ground hard. I tuck and roll, my messenger bag slapping me in the face repeatedly. Blood fills my mouth. I pull my arm up to cover my face, but I'm rolling too fast. I slide to a stop and stand wobbling, trying to focus.

The man doesn't look big enough to drive a truck. He pulls a rusted door open for me to climb in. Frantic, I run, half diving, clutching my bag tight. Before I even know what's happening, he's behind the wheel, popping the clutch.

"Are you the Reclamation Specialist?" I ask, breathlessly.

White hair flops on his head as he nods.

I squeeze my bag and stare at the road ahead. I can't see the Landions, but I know they're out there. I know they're everywhere. Thousands of them waiting to snatch this truck up with their hissing and ticking.

The truck lurches forward. Big storm clouds roll across the sky. The road is bumpy, and the wind howls. I look out the back window, searching for Spanky and Mr. Wibbles. A nagging fear ties my thoughts in knots. Sentences fall apart in my head before they form.

The strange man asks, "Do you have the clock piece?"

The question makes me nervous. I look over. The way he squeezes the steering wheel and refuses to make eye contact makes me scoot closer to the door.

Shooptee is odd. Ursula menacing. Spanky and Mr. Wibbles are flat-out weird, but none give me the creeps.

After a second, I say, "No. I hid it back at the farm."

Snapping his head around he hisses, "What?"

"You heard me." Blue-haired girls from Baltimore don't stutter.

"Well, that changes things." The tone of his voice makes my skin crawl.

Slowly and secretly, I undo a buckle on my bag.

The truck's tires bounce over deep grooves, scraping the bottom. The landscape rolls out before us, empty and unfamiliar.

"Tell me what you did with the piece," he growls.

"It belongs to my grandmother, not you, and I'll do what I want." Except I don't want to admit that I don't even have the piece. I don't even know what it looks like. I think it must be that thing Granddaddy found in the barn but it must have fallen out of my bag.

Glaring from the side of his eye, he growls, "Is that so?"

I fear being swallowed up by the dark, but I am not afraid of bullies. Not now. Not ever. "Why bother to show up and help me if all you're going to do is be mean?"

Cutting his eyes and gunning the engine, the truck lurches across the stretch of dirt.

I *have* to get out.

Knots in my stomach churn into a deep, unsettling feeling. The landscape outside the truck is totally unfamiliar. If I run, I have no idea where I'm going. That freaks me out. The cracked side view mirrors show a crumbling world descending into darkness.

Like a glorious sign, the moles with aviator goggles stand off to the side. Montford waves a clipboard desperately.

The strange man jerks the wheel of the truck, smashing down on the accelerator.

I scream, eyes glued to the moles, who flee in all directions. Loose rocks spin out from under the tires. Moles dive headfirst into a hole. I watch them disappear one by one. The most alarming part isn't that the awful man is trying to drive over the moles.

The most alarming part is that Montford has the courage to glance back over his shoulder and scream, "Run! You've been fooled. He's a Landion!"

The moment I've been trying to avoid has finally arrived. I can hardly believe such a claim. I keep my eyes glued on Montford until he disappears headfirst down the hole. Then, I whip my head around to confront the awful man.

Except he's gone.

In the driver's seat is a hissing, ticking Landion.

Chapter Twenty-Eight

I scream and throw myself against the door. Squeezing my bag tight, I pull the handle repeatedly, but it's jammed. The Landion hisses, its black, shiny eyes threatening to swallow me alive. Reaching out its strange, bug-like hand, it pushes my face against the window. My cheek presses into the glass as tears fill my eyes. Pushing harder and harder, he's trying to hurt me, but suddenly I realize this might be what I need to get the door open. I hold the handle up and push back the scream that fills my lungs. I miss my mom. She could hold off an entire army of Landions with a shovel. I miss my room. I miss Totsie.

Finally, the Landion pulls his hand from my face, reaching for my bag. In that split second when the pressure is removed, the lock clicks, and before he has time to lay a sharp finger on my bag, the door swings open. I hang on the door, dangling from the armrest. Rocks hit my boots and knees. I hold on for a split second. I have no plan. I need a plan. I have no plan.

Huge and hunched over, the Landion reaches straight for me.

I squeeze my eyes shut tight.

My body hangs from the door, arms burning. The truck speeds over the barren landscape. A single thought repeats in my head, *let go. Let go. Let go.*

It's the only choice I have if I want to live. I am so afraid to let go. I cannot let go. I feel his sharp bug-hand graze my cheek.

I let go.

My feet slam into the ground. I tuck and roll fast, my messenger bag coming off as I somersault through dust. My arms and chin are smacked against the earth as I try to get control.

There is only one truth in my mind.

This is real. I am the only one who can do this. I will have to save myself.

Rolling to a stop, I am so dizzy when I stand up that I fall back over. Coughing up a mouthful of dust, I watch up ahead as the truck slams on its brakes, sliding to a stop. Seconds. I have seconds to come up with a plan.

The brake lights flash. I swing away from the tire tracks, grab my bag, and run. Behind me, the gears grind, and gravel sprays out from under the tires. The truck is turning. I don't have to look back to know. I cannot outrun the truck. That's a fact. Just when the heat of the engine is almost on me, a little voice yells, "Run for the hole!"

I scream over the roaring engine. "I won't fit!"

Then, just like in a movie, an army of Landions appears on the horizon. Tears press into my eyes, blurring my view. I know they're headed straight for me.

Just as the truck bumper is about to smack into my back, I scream, "What do I do?"

"Dive," Montford yells back.

Knowing I'm toast if this doesn't work, I dive headfirst into the ground. Small rocks and sand fill my mouth.

"Run!" Montford yells from somewhere up ahead.

Shaking off my disorientation, I spit out a mouthful of dirt and realize I'm inside a tunnel. Sand rubs against my teeth. Light pours in from the top of the hole. Bright light and the terrifying rumble of the truck.

"Run!" Montford yells again.

Footsteps pound above. Dirt crumbles on my head. Fear surges through my brain. Within seconds, a giant Landion hand swoops down, grazing the top of my head, and that's all I need to run. The Landion rips up a huge piece of earth. Dirt floods the tunnel. I can't see Montford anymore. I tumble and fall forward, wading through loose dirt, climbing over mounds forming on my path. Again, the hand grazes my head. I don't know why the absolute danger of all this hasn't fully set in. I am dealing with other worlds filled with giants who are going to turn back time. That he's trying to grab my head lets me know full well that this does not end well if I don't do something.

Shifting my messenger bag to my back, I duck away from his hand and climb over the mounds until I reach the path ahead. There, I run for my life. I run with a surge of strength into another tunnel, growing darker by the second. Footsteps thunder above my

150

head. I don't know how much farther I can go before the whole thing collapses. Loose dirt burns my eyes.

Suddenly, up ahead, I hear Montford yell, "Here! Run faster."

For a split second, that whiny voice inside my head wants to stop and beg him to save me.

If I live long enough.

A pile of dirt collapses. It's too big to run around.

That awful hand reaches down.

Instinctively, I push backward. Dirt surrounds me on all sides, a great hole swallowing me alive. I am just about to spin around and try to run in the opposite direction when a small mole hand reaches through the dirt. Its big, wide palm feels strange, but I grab it, and it pulls me to the other side. It's still dark, but farther down the tunnel I see the elevator flooded with light.

Montford scampers in front of me, running out of breath. I run for the elevator. Just as I am about to stumble through the shiny metal doors, that horrible hand grabs hold of me. I throw my body forward and watch as the entire hunk of land is ripped open above me.

It looks like one inspirational photo where clouds part and the sun smiles. A Landion's face fills the hole. His awful, razor-sharp insect teeth swoop down.

Montford shrieks.

Falling forward into the elevator, I feel myself snatched up by my left foot.

"No!" Montford yells, grabbing onto the cuff of my hoodie.

The Landion dangles me upside down. Blood and panic rush to my brain. The Landion lifts me straight up to his mouth, black eyes glowing, mouth ticking and hissing.

"Give me the clock piece, girl child. You'll never save the humans. They had all the time in the world to save themselves."

"It doesn't belong to you," I scream back, feeling faint from terror. The way to get over a fear of the dark is by coming face to face with a Landion. Fifteen feet tall, certainly angry, I dangle in front of his mouth, which smells like car exhaust. My nostrils burn from dirt, a gasping, suffocating feeling in my throat, too dry to swallow.

Running a sharp insect finger down my arm until it bleeds, it hisses, "You're all going to die."

Maybe that's the truth.

Maybe the end is near.

Maybe is still maybe.

He opens his mouth wide and pulls me close, my face bumping into his lip. I open my own mouth wide and bite down hard. A great hiss escapes his mouth. For the briefest second, he lets go. I push off with my feet and fall away from his body. Down, down, down I fall, into the hole of dirt.

Montford yells from my sleeve. "When we hit the ground, run for the elevator."

After hitting the ground, I stumble face first into the elevator. Behind me, the doors close. Relaxing music clicks on. I am covered,

152

head to toe, in dirt. I've never been so happy to see moles in all my life. Montford wrestles himself from my sleeve, dusting his soft fur off with his big hands.

Quietly, he picks up his spear and cocks his head, blinking. "I don't remember saying goodbye."

"I don't remember saying goodbye, either." I whisper.

Chapter Twenty-Nine

Clods of dirt fall to the stone floor as I step out of the elevator. Seven sets of seven moles, all wearing aviator goggles, stare at me, heads tilted.

One mole asks, "How is she using the doorways?"

"Because she has the clock piece," Montford says.

"The what? No—she couldn't."

"Yes," Montford says. "That's why this has been so confusing."

"I thought her grandmother had the clock piece," another mole says.

Montford shakes his head. "I took the piece back to the crow."

Personally, I am too exhausted to argue with moles. Video games have epic events where you collect supplies and stamina, but what no one tells you is they need a nap mode. "I don't think I have the clock piece, guys." It's just a guess, but I'm pretty sure they think I'm more connected than I really am.

Another mole asks, "What about her mother?"

"My mother is in Afghanistan." I lean against the wall, laying my cheek against the cool stone.

All the moles look at each other, shaking their heads.

"The secret was passed by the crow," Montford says.

"This is a strange turn of events," one mole says. "How could he have found her?"

"I think he was in the barn," Montford says.

Another one chimes in, "She is in the gravest danger."

Montford pinches his lips tight and his whiskers bunch up. "Don't you see," he says grimly, "if we don't help her, then she'll never be able to accomplish her task."

"Oh, my—"

"Oh, dear—"

I furrow my brow tight and notice blood on the stones. "Guys," I say, because I haven't seen a single girl mole.

"We must get her to the switching station."

"That is forbidden."

"It doesn't matter," Montford says, walking quickly in my direction. "Forbidden or not. I will risk it."

If only I could close my eyes just for a second. Just one teeny, tiny second. Figuring everything out on my own is exhausting.

One of the moles points to my blood dripping down onto the stone. "You should have told us the Landion scratched you."

I look down at my arm where a long scratch drips blood. "I— well, I didn't know."

"The Landions are not filled with blood, they're filled with poison."

My arm throbs. "What?"

"The only known antidote to their poison is carried by the Reclamation Specialists."

My stomach twists and turns. I push away from the stone wall. I stumble forward, whispering, "I don't think I can do this." A wave of dizziness throws me sideways into a door. The wood shudders as I try to hold myself upright.

Pushing at my heels, Montford insists, "We really must go now."

I stumble down the hall to a door with boards nailed across the front. *DO NOT ENTER* is painted across the wood. *No trespassing. Turn back now. Private entry.* All these messages scrawled across the wooden surface. The last one gives me the shivers.

This might be the last door you enter.

Ever.

Turn back now.

I pinch my face up tight, the way I do when I'm not in the mood to deal with reality. "What about the Landions?"

Montford looks up at me, his eyes glistening in the lamplight. "Haven't you figured out insects are the exception to a few rules?"

I frown. "That's not fair."

"Look, insects have a lot to deal with. Being the exception to a few rules ensures their survival."

My eyes narrow. I want to be the exception.

Montford gestures for me to open the door full of warnings that instruct me not to open, so I am understandably hesitant and dizzy. An awful hissing blasts through the tunnels.

"They're going to find us," Montford whispers, urgently.

An angry, seething wind hisses past my face. I put one glitter green combat boot against the stone and pull at the board with my hands. I am so sleepy, so ready to take a nap. I pull and pull until the board breaks apart in my hand. Splinters of wood fly into the air as I fall back to the stone. Montford does not give up on me. He rushes to my side and pushes me up.

I wobble like the world is spinning. What a strange, wobbly, spinning world I think, falling forward to turn the knob. The soft wood crumbles in my hand.

"Keep going," Montford urges.

Moles with goals.

Loops making leaps.

Giving the door a good shove, boards splinter apart and I fall into an old, dusty room. Curtains shiver as the door bangs against the wall. Inside, tables stacked with maps fill the space, with desk lamps lighting the small room. Strange, dark tunnels lead out from all four corners. The shimmering light of sunset glimmers in the panes. That horrible hiss screams through the tunnel behind me.

"You must get inside," Montford yells.

I half stumble, half run into the room. Looking left, then right, like I had to do in B-more, I slam the door and make a run for a chair. My eyes search for snakes or Landions or anything else that seeks to bring about the demise of a blue-haired girl from Baltimore before I have a chance to level up. I don't make it to the chair. I don't make it that far. I feel like I am floating until I smack into the wood floor. The fall should hurt, but I'm too tired to move. My eyes want to close, even though I want them to stay open.

Through one of the tunnel openings, a man in a suit with a funny bowler hat walks into the room. He's blurry around the edges, and I try to focus, but my eyes are crossed. He walks right up to me and jabs something into my arm. Of all the things that have happened over the last few days, this one makes me feel the most uneasy.

I open my mouth to yell, but I can't get a sound louder than a croak. "What was that?"

"The only known antidote to Landion poison."

My stomach feels like I'm on the ocean. I wobble and roll over. "Who are you?" It's a funny thing to ask. I am sure I don't know him or where I am. I hope he doesn't turn into a snake, or swallow my head, because I'm too weak to get away.

Kneeling in front of me, he says, "I am a Reclamation Specialist. I understand you're in possession of the clock piece."

Dizziness, fatigue, hunger, confusion, and outright suspicion all conspire to make me wonder what I should admit to possessing. If I admit to this man in the suit that I have the piece in my messenger bag and he turns out to be a complete or partial liar, then I have a whole new set of problems on my hands. And, right now, I've got enough problems. Like, *enough.* I got a whole list of people to save, and this big, long, confusing journey is not helping me trust new people. *Not at all.* I mean, some are trustworthy, like Shooptee, but he's always trying to get rid of me without helping, which feels a little shady.

The Reclamation Specialist leans closer, waiting. Not anxious or urgent. Patient, awaiting an answer.

"You can understand I don't want to tell anyone whether I do or not, right?"

He nods slowly. "I can." Calmly, he pauses. "But I have to know, because that changes a few things."

"Like what?"

"It changes what I will tell you. It changes what you can know. It gives me a lot more power to help you."

I'm still not sure. "You won't eat me or drop me in a pit, or destroy all mankind, will you?"

A quick laugh escapes his mouth and the suddenness shocks me, then makes me smile.

Extending his hand, he pulls me to my feet and guides me to a big, comfortable chair.

Crossing my fingers and squeezing my eyes shut, I whisper, "Yes. I have the clock piece. My grandfather found it in the barn. But I didn't know what it was when I took it."

Inhaling sharply, he reaches for another chair and pulls it close. Taking a seat in front of me, he says, "That changes everything. I am going to tell you all the things you do not know."

"What is this place?" I ask.

"It's a switching station."

"What is that?"

"It's like a pocket in time, where you can go in any direction."

"To any world?"

"You haven't been moving between worlds. You've been moving through time. In your world, you call them time slips. You think it's a different place, but it's really just a different time."

"So, the Landions are in a different time?"

Rolling his chair back a little, he opens a drawer, pulling out a file folder. "Well, for starters, time isn't what you think. Humans think of time in terms of one hour leading to the next, one minute to the next minute; like a forward march."

Convinced I will not be eaten or destroyed, I have a moment to push back on my elbows and take in my surroundings. The switching station is very old, with big, heavy wooden desks and wooden chairs with huge metal rollers. Big black phones sit on desks. Like the phones at Granddaddy's house with shiny handles you hold to your ear. Nothing like the smartphones back in Baltimore.

Shifting my messenger bag so that it sits on my lap, pieces of dirt fall to the floor. I keep my hands on top of it and ask, "So, if time doesn't move backward and forwards, then how does it work?"

"Well," he says, stopping a moment to think, "Time is everywhere. It's all around you. It can morph and change. Time is a building block of the universe, if you will."

I understand a lot of things, but I'm not sure I understand what he's saying. "So, time is like air? Invisible, but everywhere?"

"Sort of. Time is like air, like consciousness. Time is alive. You can build things with it. Worlds, for instance."

"So, time is a being?"

"No." He pulls open a clunky metal file cabinet and flips through folders.

When he doesn't elaborate, I ask, "Time is like an entity?"

Grabbing a stack of folders, he turns back to me. "Somewhat. In the beginning, a great clock was constructed. It was built to track the progression of time. It was called the Great Water Clock. A continuous, constant cycle. But then, my people figured out that by dismantling the clock, time was freed. Scientific experiment after scientific experiment showed that time, once let loose, opened all worlds to one another, creating parallel worlds that allow everything to happen all the time, all at once."

"Isn't that confusing?"

"Not if you had railed against the old ways, as my people had done. Back then, time was a road you could never turn around on."

"So, what exactly did your people do?"

"We hypothesized that by dismantling the gears to the water clock, time would no longer be contained, but instead spring alive into the universe and flow. Model after model showed it could work. We could change time. Free time from its own constraints. It was the greatest scientific discovery my people ever devised. We were

161

also nervous. We couldn't figure out if time was like a glue. If we dismantled it, would everything fall apart?"

"But it didn't," I say excitedly, because this is the first answer I've been sure about in a long time.

"True," he nods, "it did not fall apart. Once time was freed, it was no longer subject to the old laws, and a new era was born. Things could happen simultaneously, in two places at once; particles could become waves, waves could become particles. An instant fluidity was born, and all worlds that existed separately suddenly opened to each other. My people had long collected scientific data that pointed to the existence of multiple universes, but we could never locate or access them. The reason we couldn't find them was because if the water clock was locked, so were all the worlds. So my people dismantled the ancient clock, and the water poured forth and created the River of Great Divide."

"So, why aren't the Landions mad at you? If it was your scientific experiments that created this mess then why don't they come after you?"

"My home and my world were destroyed by the Landions thousands of years ago. Only the Reclamation Specialists escaped capture because we were out in the field when it happened. There are five of us left. We have spent millennia trying to prevent the Landions from collecting all the pieces of the clock. We are down to the last piece, and rumor has it, it was passed to your grandmother, who hid it, and then to the crow who found it."

"I don't know about everything you're saying, but I do know I desperately need to get to the other side of the River of Great Divide."

In the warm room with the buttery light, the Reclamation Specialist puts his hands together, palms flat, squeezes tight a few seconds before pulling them apart. There, in the center of his hands, is a holographic image of me with Spanky and Mr. Wibbles.

Knots tighten in my stomach. "What is that?"

"This is time. Fluid. Malleable. Alive."

"But that's very different than how we see time."

"Exactly. Which is why you're accessing doors in the tunnels built by the moles, and I'm moving back and forth through time trying to get an angle on all this. For some reason, when the clock was dismantled it created a closed, time-like curve for certain individuals. Once you are able to access fluid time, it loops you back around to the starting point. But our math was off, and now, I think you're stuck in a causal loop. Our meddling has created a giant puzzle we all have to figure out."

My whole brow pinches tight at the intersection of science and math. "What's a causal loop?"

"Well, it's—it's something that we probably shouldn't have been playing with like a toy. It's like an event that causes another event that loops back in time to cause the original event."

"Oh, my god," I blurt out. "The maps."

The Reclamation Specialist raises his eyebrows. "The what?"

"The maps," I say. "The maps my grandmother was always drawing."

"Oh, yes," he says, suddenly, like we're speaking the same foreign language.

My grandmother collected maps.

Drew maps.

Studied maps.

She laid them on tops of counters and tables.

In the fading twilight, on the corner of the porch, she drank coffee and stared at maps. Until she vanished. The maps were always looping back around to the same spots.

In that small room with buttery yellow light, I pull out her maps. Opening to the center pages, I lay them out. The Reclamation Specialist leans forward, eyes scanning the pages, one by one.

Finally, he scans the last one and says, "These are all the routes we already tried. I was told you'd be in the possession of some new map. Something cleverly disguised."

"This is all I have."

"Did you see anything else?"

I shrug. "I don't know what I'm looking for."

The room feels so safe, and the question takes me back to wanting to stuff myself into the back of my closet and hide. He presses the hologram flat like an accordion.

"I think that…" my voice trembles. "How is Wibbles alive?" I ask, because it's the one thing I've been wanting to ask since I saw him with Spanky.

"Things show up differently in different timelines. Particles and waves are only variants of perception, and time is a master manipulator of matter."

"So, Wibbles is alive in this timeline, but a stuffed animal in another."

"Mr. Wibbles is Mr. Wibbles. How you see him is what changes."

"So, I'm different in every timeline?"

"You're human. You are the only species that's exactly the same in every timeline. You cannot shapeshift or alter your reality. In some ways, it is limiting. In other ways, you are the only species that shows up as a carbon copy in every timeline. You are the only species that can be real and exact in every timeline."

"So, there are more people like me?"

"You are the race of Loops. A special breed that learned to adapt and move through the quantum field in different ways than other humans. Loops making endless leaps to save your world. You are the descendants of Handsome Lake, the most famous Lakota, who learned that time is alive."

"Then why is my mom in Afghanistan? Why isn't she choosing pennies from enormous, talking snakes?"

"Because the loop leaps and skips a generation."

"You're making that up."

"I'm totally serious. Science and magic are more similar than we'd like to admit."

My brow furrows. "Then, which Loop am I?"

165

"Well, I hope you're the Loop that succeeds."

"What, exactly, is your job?"

"We specialize in reclamation of all kinds. I can only see how to help you from our own timelines, and that's why none of us can give you all of the pieces at once. I can help you get back so that you reclaim your power. It is imperative you accept my help. The Landions don't want to just get rid of humans, they want to destroy the Loops. Those bodies in that mound behind your farm are from Landions, a long time ago. Giants who roamed your Earth. It was Handsome Lake who saved your people and put an end to their terror. They want nothing more than to return."

"Can the Landions get to the farm? Can they get to Granddaddy?"

"Right now, without the completion of the water clock, they can only send shadows."

The shadows in the field. "Are the shadows real?"

"They are like impressions. *Real. Not real.* But they will get through eventually if we don't stop them. The only advantage that you have is Landions cannot enter your time since the shaman locked them out."

"Can't I just hide the last piece and be done with it?"

"No, because the Landions are a military race."

"What does that mean?"

"It means that every Landion is a soldier. Because their bloodline is insect they can travel through time. They are master manipulators. They will never stop. Hundreds of thousands of them searching all day, every day. We'll all find ourselves right back here if we try and avoid them now."

"But that doesn't seem normal. Why would an entire race of beings want to destroy another?"

"How many extinctions has the human race brought about?"

"But—"

"How many?"

There, in the warm room, I feel foolish, tired, and old. Way older than my eleven years. At that moment, I am being called to account for every bad human decision, and I'll say this: *I don't like it one bit.* "You can't say we're all bad," I offer, half-heartedly.

"And I can't say you're all good."

A deep sadness grabs hold of me, tightening my gut.

"Don't worry," he sighs loudly, rolling back in his chair. "My people weren't so good, either. That's how we dwindled to five with no fixed place in time. These switching stations are our only home, really."

"Will you ever be able to go back to your original home?"

"Home is no longer an option. The Landions destroyed our entire timeline, cracked it into pieces. I move through time as a free agent."

"Well, if we survive this, then come to the farmhouse for dinner. We'll have canned peas and instant mashed potatoes."

Laying his hand on the desk, he stands. "First things first. Take a deep breath. When you exit the switching station you're going to have to do this, and you're going to have to do it alone."

I stand up, adjusting my messenger bag. The dizziness has passed. I feel like I could run all the way to the Corner Market for a bag of mini powdered doughnuts. This blue-haired girl from Baltimore extends her hand to shake. "You saved my life," I say. "Thank you."

"Don't thank me yet. Remember, reality divides you. Time divides you. Yet all the while you are real and can't see your true power. Loops draw the leaps. Leaps open doors."

I nod and step into the nearest tunnel. It's dark and I can't see where I'm going. I turn back around to ask the Reclamation Specialist where I'm going, but my mouth is filled with water and I can't breathe.

Chapter Thirty

Freezing water engulfs me as I try to take a breath. I look up. Light reflects off the surface. Thrusting my arms out to the side, I swim straight up. The weight of my wet clothes and bag pull me towards the bottom, but I've gotta have air, so I double down and really swim. My arms pump the water hard. I'm pushed along so swiftly by the current that I finally break the surface.

I have just enough time to suck in a breath, cough out a mouthful of water, and hear Wibbles scream, "You're alive!" before being pulled under again.

I fight my way back to the top, prepared to suck in a breath this time. I can't let go of my bag, but I pull it around to the front of my body so it's not dragging me down.

My face breaks the surface and I gasp for air. Spanky is right next to me. From where I am in the river I can see the shore.

Spanky and Mr. Wibbles thrash around next to me, yelling. I try to rise above the choppy water. I pump my arms hard in the freezing water, fighting the current.

Spanky and Mr. Wibbles pop up near my head.

"Float," Wibbles yells.

"I can't—" I gulp water, slipping under the surface a second, then popping back up.

"Press your bag to your stomach," Spanky yells, "and float."

Floating is easier than it sounds. Floating means letting go.

Floating also means staying alive, and I don't have a ton of choices.

"Push with your arms," Spanky yells. Next thing I know, Wibbles is on my other side, tugging at my arm.

"Try and float over to the shore."

Sounds easy.

#isn't

My glitter-green combat boots and messenger bag weigh me down, but there is no way I'm giving up, either. The force of the river swirls us in circles, but if I use my arms as I spin it pushes us closer to shore.

Not a perfect plan, but a plan.

Trees line the river, green and lush. A sandy shore runs along both sides. Landions could be hiding, but I don't see any. It doesn't matter. I have to get us out of this freezing water, because even with the roar of the river I can still hear Wibbles' teeth chattering.

The current spins me around, sending me closer to shore.

Spanky squeezes my arm and yells, "Look!"

Not too far away, a fallen tree sticks out over the surface. I pump my arms and spin, trying to get close enough to grab onto a limb.

Kicking hard with my legs, I struggle to the branch. Spanky slaps at the water, reaching for my hand. Wibbles grabs onto my hoodie floating on the surface behind me.

"Hold on tight to me," I yell.

I spin and use my arms to guide until my knee bumps into the wet bark, and I swing my arms, holding tight. Pulling myself out of the river isn't an option. My boots and bag feel like they weigh a thousand pounds. Wedging myself against the tree, I hold on and move sideways towards the shore.

I've never been so happy to feel mud under my boots in all my life. Pushing upright, the weight of the river, my wet clothes, and the absolute trauma of nearly drowning threaten to pull me back down. Spanky and Wibbles catch a ride to shore holding onto a shoulder. My boots are so heavy I stumble across the sand and fall to one knee. Spanky jumps down, trying to catch his breath. I know I don't have time to stop, so I flip open my messenger bag. Water leaks from the sides. The flame of a fiery arrow sparkles inside.

"Wow. Impressive," I say.

"What do you have in there?" Wibbles asks.

"Some honeysuckle juice and fiery arrows, a bow, and a really wet sketchbook."

Spanky pinches up his face. "We need to find where they've taken everyone."

"I know." I stand and watch water squish out of my boots. It's enough to make me sigh. Me and these boots got a history.

"Come on," Wibbles says, shimmying down my arm, hitting the ground running.

Spanky looks up at me. "He's right."

I spend the next few minutes shaking and squeezing water from my clothes and bag.

Wibbles watches and fidgets.

He got that from me.

Or maybe I got that from him.

Either way, we take off running.

Since Landions were in the forest on Shooptee's side, I search with my eyes as we run. The forest that runs along the water's edge is quiet.

That makes me nervous.

I'm still wet and running makes me feel like I'm carrying fifty pounds.

The only good part is:

a) we're not ambushed, and,

b) I'm running so fast my clothes are drying.

So, that's something.

Finally, we cut through the trees to where the edge of the water meets the desert. The desert is absolutely enormous. It goes on for as far as the eye can see.

"Hurry," Spanky says.

I totally agree. We need to hurry. *But to where?*

This desert goes on so far there's nothing to tell us where to go. No landmarks or anything.

Behind us is the river, but in front of us, a sort of mind-boggling insanity.

"Where is their camp?"

Spanky shrugs.

Wibbles forces a smile. "I just got here."

"Me too," I say, adjusting my bag.

I start off across the open space. Maybe the only thing worse than hiking wet is hiking across sand in wet boots.

I feel complaining coming on.

I mean, normal kids are leveling up with a Snickers bar and a cold root beer.

I'd give anything for a powdered mini doughnut.

Just one.

This is what life comes down to.

Begging for one doughnut.

Not a bag.

Not a dozen.

Just one.

Spanky is swallowed in the sand as he runs. It doesn't slow him down. He emerges on the other side, like ducking through a wave.

Trees only grow along the bank, so once we've hiked out a distance it's just all desert.

Up ahead, something flashes.

"Drop to the ground," I whisper, taking my own advice.

Spanky and Wibbles hit the ground.

I hold my breath.

New hobby.

Holding my breath and hoping it isn't a trap.

"What is that?"

Spanky shields his eyes from the light with his furry hands. He squints and says, "Hey, I think that's the truck you were in earlier."

The creepy truck I had to escape.

"Can you drive?" Wibbles asks.

"I'm eleven years old."

Spanky isn't even listening. "Come on," he yells, running for the truck.

I'm taller and can run faster, so I get to the truck first.

It's still intact. The doors are still open.

"Get in," Spanky says.

We all climb in. The big steering wheel feels weird in my little hands, and I can barely reach the pedals.

"Let's go." Spanky slaps the steering wheel.

I suck in a huge breath. I've never driven anything except bumper cars at a crappy little amusement park on the outskirts of Baltimore.

Slowly, I turn the key, making a deal with myself. If it starts, I drive.

The engine roars to life.

Last time I was in this truck I had to run for my life.

Wibbles jumps to the dash and points like a great explorer. "That way."

The gears grind as I put the truck in drive. I slam my glitter-green combat boot onto the gas, and the truck lurches forward, throwing Wibbles to the seat.

"Whoa," Spanky says.

I like the feeling of racing across the desert. Trails of dust form behind us. With nothing to slow us down, I push hard on the accelerator until it hits the floor. I'm driving so fast it feels like we're flying.

No wonder adults like driving.

It's kinda awesome.

Wind blowing through the window dries my blue hair.

My tired feet get a rest.

I glance down at the dash. The speedometer is broken, but the tank is full. The truck blasts across the wide-open space and I let out a loud *whoop*.

Wibbles and Spanky hold hands on the seat.

I don't know where those awful giants have camped, but we're gonna find my friends and my grandmother, load them in the back, and drive as fast as we can back to the river. Wheels make escape a lot easier. Far off in the distance, a huge stone wall comes into view. Tall and wide, it looks like it circles a small village.

I press even harder.

We are going to do this.

We are going to get them out.

#I'MDRIVING

Totsie is gonna freak.

Wind whips up, lashing sand at the cracked windshield. Suddenly, the truck feels like it's rising up. A wall of static rises in front of the truck. I pull my foot off the gas.

The truck just keeps rising off the ground.

"Oh, no!" Spanky yells. "The Landions!"

"What? *Where?*"

"Everywhere. This is how they distort space," he yells, running for cover under my messenger bag.

Outside the truck, Landions raise up from the ground. Hundreds at first, then thousands, rising up from the earth. The entire desert is covered with them. That's why they weren't hiding in the forest. They're the same color as sand. They've been lying flat on the ground, and because they are the same color I didn't see them. I've driven too far from the river to try and outrun them.

Mr. Wibbles screams.

I slam my glitter-green combat boot on the gas, but nothing happens.

The truck doesn't move.

It's lifted higher and higher.

Until the truck is in front of the biggest Landion I've ever seen.

I reach for the only things I have—fiery arrows and honeysuckle juice.

I'm just about to pop the cork when something smacks me in the back of the head, hard.

I pull the bottle up, but the truck cab goes gray around the edges.

Spanky screams, "Noooooo—"

Chapter Thirty-One

A voice whispers in the dark. "Maya Loop?"

Cold, wet stone presses against my cheek. Moving my arm makes my entire body ache. The back of my head pounds. My eyes pop open. I am in a tiny stone box, little bigger than a bathroom. My heart beats fast. Blue-haired girls from Baltimore don't dig being held captive. I look around in the dim light from the cracks in the door. My messenger bag is gone. Dang it.

"Maya Loop," the voice whispers again.

Rolling over, I see a tiny opening in the wooden door, like a mail slot. Quickly, I pull myself upright. The pounding in my skull makes me so dizzy I fall back against the wall.

"Is that you?" the voice asks.

I brush the foggy muck from my brain and press myself against the door.

"Rowan?" I whisper back.

Clapping with a great sigh of relief echoes against the stone. "I knew it was you," he whispers excitedly.

I take a deep breath and feel along the seams for loose stones. "Where are we?"

His whisper drops low. "I don't know. After I fell off the car, they blindfolded me and brought me here."

"How long did it take?"

"I don't know, but we crossed a river. I could hear it, and smell the mud along the bank."

"Is this some kind of castle?"

"I don't think so."

"Is anyone else here?"

Rowan sucks in a breath so fast it sounds like wind in the narrow hall. "The Assassin Bug. And, I believe, your grandmother may be here with an Indian man."

If I lay on my back and press my cheek flat against the door, I can almost see the ceiling through the tiny slat.

"Why do they have your grandmother, and why do they want me? I haven't done anything. They won't even give me anything to eat. Every time I ask, they laugh."

"I'm not really sure, Rowan, but I think we might have to save our world."

"From what? These awful black-eyed bug monsters?"

"I think they might want to turn back a clock so humans never existed."

"You are the weirdest girl I've ever met," he says, and the soft rise of his voice calms my nerves briefly.

"I can accept weird. Tell me what you've learned about this place."

"I haven't been out of this tiny room."

I know I won't find it, but I feel around again in the dark for my bag. Down the hall, a metal door clangs. The sound of heavy footsteps marches in perfect time. Not sure what to do, and not a lot of time to do it, I roll away from the door, over hard stone, and pretend to be asleep. I open my eyes enough to see through my lashes.

Footsteps pound closer and closer, the stone floor shuddering from the weight. A ring of keys rattles outside my door like the chime of a dreadful clock. A second later, the door opens, and huge bug-like hands whip a canvas bag over my head.

I want to scream. I want to toss and fight as my hands and feet are squeezed. Blue-haired girls from Baltimore don't give bullies that kind of satisfaction. I also know that I can't be scratched, at least, not without the antidote which I don't currently possess. I am pulled from the stone hole and shoved into a cage. I can see out of the bottom of the canvas bag. A single Landion carries my cage in his hand, and he isn't nice about it. The cage jostles and bounces off the walls. Down the long hall I go, my heart beating fast. Quietly, I reach up and pull the canvas back. Stone hallways in both directions.

When we come to a turn that leads through a dark room into a well-lit chamber, I see huge glass booths. It's such a strange room and a strange sight. It takes me a second, but I gasp when I realize they aren't glass booths.

They are killing jars.
Huge killing jars.

Inside one is my grandmother. Inside the other is the Assassin Bug. Inside the third is a tall Indian man who I assume must be Handsome Lake. I am overwhelmed by dread. Suddenly, I know exactly where I am.

The room full of danger.

Chapter Thirty-Two

My grandmother sits slumped on the bottom; a worried look pinches her thin face. Eyes closed, mouth in a frown, she doesn't even see me.

I grab the bars of my cage and squeeze. "I'm here!" I scream. She doesn't move.

I can't tell if she's alive.

"I'm here!" I scream louder, feeling my chest shudder in that horrible way it does when I am about to cry.

The Landion jerks my cage side to side, knocking me over. I hit my head on the bars but stay upright.

On the third try, I give it my all, because I'm scared to be locked away without her seeing me. "I'm here," I scream, so loud it shakes my entire body. "I saw you on the stairs. I saw you!"

Through the bars, I can see her perfectly. Her eyes pop open and she turns, startled.

I am so happy to see her I actually wave. A silly, funny *ohmygod* you're really alive wave. My grandmother's body trembles, like she's swallowing a gulp of air, but a deep frown covers her entire face, and that makes me scared. She stands quickly but loses her balance and smacks the side of her head against the glass.

I stick my arm through the bars of my cage, reaching as far as I can, which isn't nearly far enough. A trickle of blood rolls down her temple. A deep fear starts in my gut and spreads out like a starburst. It's terrible. I reach farther and farther, too far away to ever touch the glass, but still, I press my cheek against the bars and reach.

My grandmother sways, dizzy from lack of air. The palms of her hands lay flat against the glass. The smooth lines of her fingers look like paintings.

Suddenly, the Landion drops my cage to the floor. My head bangs into the steel bars and I chip a tooth. I feel the crack, then the tiny piece hits my tongue.

The Landion unscrews the top of the enormous jar and my grandmother's eyes go wide. She inhales deep, her chest heaving as she takes in all the fresh air entering the jar.

I ignore my chipped tooth and scream, "I'm here! I'm here. I'm going to get us out."

My grandmother's face turns white, and in-between deep breaths, she yells, "Run—"

The Landion slams the lid back on the jar. My grandmother gulps air.

The Landion snatches my cage up, tossing me side to side. "Your days of running are over."

Tears fill my grandmother's eyes, and I worry she'll run out of air.

Passing by, I see the Assassin Bug, his legs on the glass, pleading.

Pleading for his life.

But, maybe, pleading for mine now.

It's the second time I've seen him trapped in a jar, and that make my heart hurt.

Handsome Lake holds my gaze. He looks so tired and weary, like he is barely held together. Dressed in animal skins and broken feathers, he looks so old, like something not of these worlds.

The Landion rounds the corner into a stone hall. Behind me, the jars aren't visible. They're stuck in jars running out of air, repeatedly. Alone. Until the clock is put back together and *poof!* We vanish. I can't think of anything more awful.

I scream, "Let me go!"

The Landion hisses loudly and laughs. It's the most menacing, darkest laugh I've ever heard.

It makes me want to cry.

I burn the look of my grandmother's face into my mind. A deep, worried look, cast in the tight pinch of too little sleep, lips twisted into a frown. And the Assassin Bug. I saved him once. I did. I saved him from a killing jar, and I can do it again.

The Landion drops my cage on the floor in the center of an enormous stone room. The giant hissing bugs are well over fifteen feet tall, but the room is at least a hundred feet tall. Amber colored stone covers the floor. It's like being swallowed alive by a huge open space. Far ahead, down the stone wall on the left, is a wooden door.

I turn to look over my shoulder. In the far back corner, there's another door, identical to the first. That's my mom's influence. Know your exits, yo. I'm in the habit of counting my steps. I'm guessing it's about a hundred and fifty steps to each door, maybe three hundred to cross the entire room. Long way if I'm running for my life. My heart beats so fast I feel like I will black out.

A breeze whirls through stone windows up above. There is no glass, but they are too high to climb and escape.

All at once I hear great screams outside the room. The horrific sound echoes. It terrifies me. Blue-haired girls from Baltimore know to keep their head. I'm not saying it's easy. I'm just saying I made it all the way across the River of Great Divide and I'm not giving up now.

Ahead, the door to the left opens and a single Landion walks in with my messenger bag hooked on one of his three fingers. His long, sturdy insect legs stride swiftly across the room and drop it just out of my reach.

He hisses, "Where is the final piece, girl child?" Sound sizzles off of his tongue, so loud and clear it makes me jump.

Saying anything is saying too much. The piece was supposed to be in my bag. Maybe it fell out in the river, or in the tunnel. Admitting I don't have the piece will not make them nicer or let us go. Staying silent gives me time to figure out an escape route. If they think I have it then at least they'll keep me alive.

Without warning, the Landion slaps my cage across the room. My face slams into the heavy bars as it smacks into the stone wall. Immediately, the cage falls over and rolls across the floor.

185

Smacking into the wall hurts, but rolling forces me to pull myself into a ball so my fingers don't get smashed between bars and floor.

I will not cry.

I will not scream.

I will not let bullies have that satisfaction. I blink back a hot tear and watch the Landion stand perfectly still in the center of the room.

"We have toyed with your people long enough," he hisses. "Your grandmother cannot be saved. We only let her live because we knew you'd come looking for her. And you are only important because we knew you'd have the clock piece."

I do not blink.

I do not whimper.

I do not move.

I am a Zen ninja battle bunny and I can do this.

I lay perfectly still on my side in my cage, feeling my eye swell.

The Landion exhales like steam released from a valve, so calm and precise it makes my skin quiver.

"I will capture all of you until I find that piece, human girl. Then, we will be done with your tainted species forever."

"You're far from perfect," I scream.

With long strides of great purpose, he walks straight to my cage and kicks it violently across the room. The bars clack against stone until, a hundred paces later, I smack the wall again.

Keeping my hands and arms pulled in tight, I bounce like a ball off the bars. The rolling makes my stomach flip, and before I can take a deep breath and hold it in, I vomit on the floor.

The Landion stares at me with contempt. "What a weak and filthy species."

With my stomach heaving, I force my eyes to stay open as the Landion crosses the room toward my cage. "Your world, and the time in which you are in it, is one of the smallest, and yet humans are the most devious. They lie right to your face. Human girl, we are so tired of your lies."

My knuckles bleed. The smell of acid rises from the floor where I threw up.

The Landion continues to advance, his words hissing and ticking. "Where is the clock piece?"

I wipe my face on my sleeve. "I destroyed it."

The Landion tosses his head back like he's going to laugh, but instead, his howling roar frightens me to the core. "Liar human. Liar human. Your entire species should be called *Homo Liarus*: Lying Man."

A tremble starts deep down in my gut. A tremble I can't stop. I need time. Time to assemble a plan, regardless of how patched-together it might be. A plan to get us back to the warm, buttery light of the farm at sunset. I want so many impossible things, and for the briefest, strangest second, I actually consider some of these might be possible. I don't know why. I'm pretty sure despair makes me cling to a miracle, because the truth is too impossible to accept. The truth that I have absolutely no idea what I'm doing. The truth that staying alive is hard.

The truth that we might all die here.

Chapter Thirty-Three

The echo of water dripping onto stone fills the tiny room. It's really just a hollowed-out cube, barely big enough to stand. A small, cold, hard box I've been left in to die. I rip a piece of my shirt off and tie it around my hand to stop the bleeding. More than ever, I know the Landions will never take pity on us, never take pity on humans. They'll search until they find the piece. The piece I never actually thought to destroy. Foolishly, I thought I could explain to the Landions how awesome mini powdered doughnuts are, or kettle corn, or the wild feeling of your stomach bottoming out on the Ferris wheel, or just how good a Scooby Doo rerun marathon can be.

Humans and Landions.

Living in harmony.

What a delusion.

Some things are meant to be destroyed.

My body aches intensely, like I've run the mile in PE for a month straight and then fallen over the edge of the world. The pinky finger on my left hand hurts, and I can't tell if the back of my head is bleeding. What a mess I've landed myself in by getting caught.

I think back to Totsie's rules in Baltimore.

Be kind.

Speak your truth.

Get loud if people refuse to listen.

"Maya Loop?" a voice whispers in the dark.

"Rowan?"

"No, this is Spanky. Have you seen Mr. Wibbles?"

"No. I only saw long, stone hallways and stone rooms and awful cages and killing jars."

"I think they're going to keep us here," Spanky's voice quivers. "Like this. Locked away."

A sharp gasp in the dark is followed by, "I think they're going to kill us." It's Rowan. The sound of his voice makes my heart skip a beat.

"They're going to erase us," I say because why bother with pretty lies when the end is near.

"They've been planning to do that for a long time," Spanky says.

"They only need one piece."

"It's not just a piece. They need a specific person. Only the Loops can restart the clock."

"They want me to build something that makes me disappear?"

Spanky sighs in the dark. "It's not like the Landions are trying to make friends."

"We have to get out of here," Rowan says urgently. "We have to."

"Do you know how to get back to the river?" I ask Spanky.

"I might be able to get back to the river, but I don't know how to get out of here."

Far off, a heavy metal door slams shut, echoing down the hall.

We fall silent.

In that second I know we must find my messenger bag. It's the only way out. It's our only hope.

Shuffling feet swish down the hall.

Keys jangle.

A second later, light floods into my cell. Shooptee stands, holding a key ring almost as big as his body.

I am stunned. "You came to get me."

He nods his furry head, opening the next stone cell. "Shooptee brave. Only Shooptee left. No time to be 'fraidy."

Rowan falls forward from his dark cell, blinking, trying to get his eyes to adjust to the light. "Hey, I know you. You drive that funny little car."

Shooptee stares up at Rowan. "Shooptee have car," he says, wiggling his furry eyebrows.

"We've got to get out of here," I say, urgently.

Shooptee toddles over to the next cell and unlocks the door. Spanky rushes out, face to face with his furry forest friend.

A great thunder of footsteps echoes through the halls.

"We have to go," I whisper.

With a little zing to his step, Shooptee turns and walks toward the end closest to us. "Shooptee know the way."

"But I'm pretty sure my grandmother and the Assassin Bug are that way," I point.

"Shooptee read prophecy many times. How many times you read?"

I look around and avoid eye contact. I didn't know there was actual reading material. "I don't think I got that memo."

Doors slam shut farther down the hall and footsteps echo. I grab Shooptee, Rowan grabs Spanky, and we run to the closest door.

"What if this is a trap," I whisper.

Shooptee's whiskers tickle my cheek as he speaks. "Not a trap."

Now I understand why he drives his fast, crazy car. Shooptee isn't particularly zippy on his own.

At the end of the hall Shooptee points left, then right, then left again, until we finally stumble through a doorway into a large, stone room. Shooptee wiggles free, sliding down my leg. "You go down steps outside. Time to run."

He turns to go back the direction we just came.

"What are you doing?"

Disappearing around the corner, he says, "Shooptee brave."

Rowan, Spanky, and I run down the steps outside. A wide ledge leads across a courtyard. Spanky is small enough to run. Rowan and I must balance the way I did back in Baltimore, on the playground beams. With tremendous haste, we cross, looking everywhere for Landions. In a blur, arrows shoot past my face. I dive headfirst down onto the ledge, hoping Rowan follows. Quickly, I crawl on my belly to the nearest window. Spanky is already there.

Grabbing my hand, he pulls me up into a room. Arrows crack into the stone next to my shoulder.

Across the room is a door with a huge piece of metal acting as a lock. The kind you simply lift to open the door.

"Help me lift the bar," I yell to Rowan. "We'll hide in here."

The metal lock is so heavy it barely budges.

"Push hard," I say, face hot, my muscles burning.

Rowan strains.

We push harder.

The metal lock moves.

Footsteps thunder across the roof. A great hiss fills the air. I suck in a deep breath and heave as hard and high as I possibly can. The lock comes loose, and the door slowly falls open.

I push Rowan and Spanky inside and quickly pull the door shut, leaving only a crack for me to see through. Outside, Landions run past. I shrink back. We must get back to the river. We need weapons and a map. This entire place is like a fortress. *Think.* I am a blue-haired girl from Baltimore who can do anything.

My eyes adjust to the dim light. Below, I see torches mounted to the walls. A single cough, way down below, lets me know we're not alone. Staring down, I realize we are standing on a stone staircase that leads down to what looks like an enormous pit. To my absolute horror, I see hundreds of Shooptees huddled together, teeth chattering, with matted, wet fur.

Sad Shooptee faces look up at me.

I gasp. "There's more than one Shooptee left."

Spanky looks out over the tired, scared faces. "So, this is where you all went," he whispers in complete surprise.

A single voice rises from the center of quivering fur. "Because we help the upright lady we get locked in here. Shooptee never learn."

Chills run up my arms, straight to my shoulders, zapping my brain. The realization makes my voice tremble. My voice rises, and the echo is so powerful it vibrates like a war cry.

"That upright lady is my grandmother, and I am going to get you out of here."

Shooptee eyes turn upward. I gaze into their sweet, shadowed faces for a split second before turning abruptly to Spanky and Rowan.

Pointing to the stone staircase that winds down to the bottom, I say, "Rowan and Spanky, take the Shooptee back to the river and get them safely to the other side." Rowan starts to protest, but I run down the steps, clapping my hands. "Quick. We've got to get out of here."

The Shooptee watch me, silent and shivering.

I lower my voice and whisper, "The Shooptee are brave."

A few cock their heads to the side.

"Brave Shooptee must get to the river," I say.

Many Shooptee blink, but none move.

"You're free," I yell.

It only takes a second before they begin filing up the concrete stairs like ants marching.

Seeing that my pep talk has worked, I turn around and run back to the door. "I have to get Shooptee. I can't leave him out there. Knowing his people are alive changes everything."

Rowan grabs my arm. "You're going to get yourself killed."

"Save your whining. I've got to find him."

Chapter Thirty-Four

The world of the Landions isn't just huge, it's enormous. Hard blocks of stone rise floor to ceiling in every hallway, every room. My mind is full of frantic thoughts. I've got to find my bag. A focus consumes my every thought. Find Shooptee. Find my messenger bag. Free my grandmother.

An arrow whizzes past my head. I duck, hopping over a short wall that looks like it's part of a drainage system. I slide to the bottom, and before anyone can spot me, I roll off and hide behind a bush.

Let me count all the times I do not have to hide behind a bush.

Shooptee pops his head around the other side. "You lazy."

I turn, shocked to hear his voice. "You're not the only Shooptee left," I blurt out.

His furry cheeks look back over his shoulder. Then, a second later, he looks back at me. "What you mean?"

I pop my head out of the bush and look around for Landions on the move. Satisfied we haven't been seen, I lower my head. "There were hundreds of Shooptee locked in a stone pit."

"You leave them locked? That not good friend."

"Spanky took them," I point through the branches, "that way. But that doesn't really seem like the way to the river." I point in the opposite direction. "Maybe that way. Hard to tell."

Shooptee's eyes go wide, and before I can say a word he runs out of the bush. Frantically, I climb out behind him and watch in horror as he hoists his furry butt up the side of a stone wall. At the top, he swings his little legs over and stands on the wall. Looking in all directions, his eyes scan the desert until his hands fly out to his sides, and he screams.

Not keen on drawing attention, I whisper, "*Shhhhh*—" but don't leave the safety of the bush.

Bouncing and pointing, he yells, "Not the only Shooptee left."

Told you so.

"Shooptee survive!"

Bouncing up and down, his knees bend, and an arrow whizzes right over his head. Thrusting his whole body backwards to avoid the arrow, he falls off the wall and rolls to a stop next to the bush. Grunting and woozy, he dusts sand from his fur and stands up. I scoop him up in my arms and pull him into the bush. I don't have time to stand around hashtagging and high-fiving because we are going to have to make a run for it.

Shooptee makes a strange little bumpy noise as I hold him in my arms and run for the stone buildings, one of which has my grandmother and the others.

"Room full of danger scary," he whispers.

Agreed, but I don't have time to feel fear. I've got to get us out of the open and find shelter.

He yells, "Dare!"

I'm confused. "Now is not the time to take a dare."

"No. Dare." He points directly at a door.

It probably leads to a room full of people who want to kill us. This is my humble experience.

"Oh, you mean 'there'," I say.

"Dare. Dare." He twists and turns in my arms, jostled by me running. "*Shoop shoop shooptee dare!*"

The Shooptee I found in his little car was curious, but a little depressed. This is an all-new version of my favorite tree dweller. Quickly, I fling the door open and run inside.

Flomp Flomp Flomp

Arrows hit the door behind us. I drop the big metal lock into place and keep running. No time to catch my breath. The hall straight ahead is dim but there are doors on both sides. They're all a blur as I run full speed with Shooptee wiggling and jiggling, soft and kinda heavy. I duck into a hall on the right and keep running. Turn, run, turn, run. Shooptee makes a gaspy sound, and I stop for half a second.

"Do you know where we are?" I wheeze.

Whiskers twitching, he looks left, then right. Finally, he says, "Shooptee know."

"Alright then, get us back to the room full of danger."

He shivers, then points. "Dat way."

The thundering echo of footsteps pounds through the halls, echoing against stone walls.

"Dare!"

I suck in my deepest breath yet and pray I reach the killing jars in time to save everyone. I round the corner and stop. There in front of me are the towering jars. *The awful, awful killing jars.* My eyes sweep across all three and see that everyone is still alive. I set Shooptee on the floor and run to my grandmother.

My grandmother is slumped on the bottom of the jar, knees pulled up, forehead resting on top.

Please, please, please let her still have air, I pray as I run over. I pound on the glass with my fists. Her head shoots up but it takes a few seconds for her eyes to focus.

I pound again, and yell, "How do I get you out of here?"

Launching herself forward, she pushes up to her feet, but only makes it a few steps before falling forward into the glass. Smacking her forehead on the glass, little drops of blood splatter near my hand. I gasp in horror, unable to help. She looks up at me with blood trickling down her brow.

"How do I get you out of here," I yell.

Her eyes drift to the top. A metal lid screwed tight. The Landions are so tall all they have to do is unscrew it. I will have to figure out a way to climb a glass jar. Which doesn't look easy. I look around for a ladder, a chair, *anything.*

My grandmother pleads on the other side of the glass, "Hurry!" I can't really hear her. She's just mouthing the word. One word. Two syllables. The line between life and death. I back up and stare straight at the top.

Shooptee waddles around, tapping at the jar with the Assassin Bug inside.

Knock them over, I hear him whisper, the same way I heard him when he was trapped back at Rowan's house.

Backing up a few more steps, I run toward the glass and slam my hands against the side. My palms sting with the force. The jar wobbles. I back up even more and get a good running start. I slam my shoulder into the jar hard and it wobbles again.

"Keep a lookout," I yell to Shooptee.

"Shooptee look."

I give it a good run once more and slam into the glass. This time the bottom of the jar spins in a circle, going round and round. Using the momentum, I keep pushing hard. A look of shock forms on my grandmother's face. The jar tips backward. Smeared blood on her forehead looks like warpaint. I keep my palms flat on the glass, pushing and pushing, grunting, until her jar tips over, knocking into Handsome Lake's jar, which knocks into the Assassin Bug's jar. The bottoms all lift and roll, pausing for seconds in mid-air, then smack the stone floor with a loud crack.

Shooptee claps his furry hands and runs to the lid. Both of us grab and twist as my grandmother crawls to the top. Once we unscrew the lid my Grandmother sucks in a huge breath, reaching for my hand. When my palm meets hers, I squeeze tight and pull. I just never in my life thought I'd be pulling her from a jar.

"Oh my god, Maya." She stumbles to her feet, pulling me in for the tightest hug ever. "We have to get the others and get out of here now."

Woozy from lack of air, she follows me to the next jar. Holding onto my shoulder, she sorta falls against the glass using her weight to twist the lid and free Handsome Lake. Inside the jar, he tumbles forward, but regains his balance and heads for the top. I run for the Assassin Bug. He's at the glass, hands on the side, waiting.

"*Hurry.*"

The huge jars make him look tiny at the bottom.

A sharp pain stings in my shoulder. After three tries, the lid turns. A look of pinched worry and hopeful anticipation on the face of the Assassin Bug keeps me going. I brace my forearms against the metal and turn until the lid comes loose and smacks the floor. Shooptee runs for the lid and drags it out of the way.

The Assassin Bug walks out of the jar, inhaling, "I knew you'd come. I knew you wouldn't give up."

Someone grabs my arm and I turn to see my grandmother and Handsome Lake.

"We have to make a run for it."

I put the Assassin Bug on my shoulder, then I pick Shooptee up. His soft, furry hands hold my hoodie tight.

"This way," my grandmother says, running for a hall on the other side of the room.

"I think this leads to a courtyard," the Assassin Bug says.

Shooptee lays his ears back and pinches up the fur around his nose. "Room full of danger bad."

Chapter Thirty-Five

Handsome Lake slows to a stop in the hallway, laying a hand on the stone wall. "I can't," he whispers, trying to catch his breath.

"We have to keep going," my grandmother urges.

"Just a minute," he exhales, like he can't get enough air in his lungs. "You have to leave me here. I am the one who started the war with them."

My grandmother turns to me fast. "Do you have the clock piece?"

"I think I had it. Granddaddy found it in the barn and I took it with me."

"Where is it now?"

I shrug, shifting a heavy Shooptee to my other arm. "It was in my messenger bag, but it must have fallen out because the Landions searched my bag. I didn't know it was the clock piece."

"You lost it?"

"Losing it is a good thing, right?" I shrug, forcing a smile. "I mean, then no one can use it against us."

Shooptee twists around in my arms, interrupting, "Shooptee have."

"What?" I ask. "How did you get the clock piece."

"Shooptee take from bag."

"You stole from me?"

Shooptee lays his ears back, whiskers twitching. "Hardly stole. Everyone know about clock piece."

My grandmother touches his fur softly. "He did the same thing to me. That way, if you don't succeed, the moles can take it back to our time."

I frown, looking directly into his furry face. "You should have told me."

Waving my insistence away he says, "Shooptee have big job."

My grandmother asks, "So where is the clock piece?"

His bushy, soft eyebrows flutter as he blinks. "In my car."

"What!" the Assassin Bug says.

"Oh, no," Handsome Lake says.

"You mean it's way back at the tree?" I ask.

"Here," Shooptee says proudly. "Have here."

"How did you get across the river?" I ask.

He cocks his head like I'm crazy. "Shooptee car fly."

"You have a flying car?" And other things I never thought I'd say out loud.

"Your car no fly?" he asks curiously.

"I'm from Baltimore. We take the bus."

Suddenly, my grandmother falls against the wall. Handsome Lake hooks his arm under hers. He's barely able to stand himself, but we all stick together. End of the world #squadgoals.

"Are you okay?"

Her head hangs in a way that scares me. Exhausted, unable to even lift a hand, she just leans into Handsome Lake, who leans into the wall. "No, I am not okay."

"What else do you need?" I ask quickly, because I know we have little time left.

Staring down the hall like she's looking back at a far-off time none of us can see, she takes a deep breath and says, "I should have never left those maps or clues. I should have never brought you all here. Most of all, I should have never put you in this kind of danger. I can't believe I've done this."

Feeling the even in and out of Shooptee's chest against mine calms me and makes me sad at the same time. Small and hardy, sweet and curious.

"It wasn't you who told me to come here," I say to my grandmother. "It was the Assassin Bug."

"We're all in this because of me," Handsome Lake says, firmly. "I'm the one who locked the Landions out of our world. They were killing our people. It wasn't like they gave me much choice. Still, I didn't harm them. I just closed our world off."

"Well, we always have a choice," my grandmother says. "I certainly had the choice to not look for you after I found your maps buried in the yard where I dug my flower beds."

"Is that why they can't use the doors? Because you locked them out?"

Handsome Lake nods his head. "I locked them out of time. It's why they exist on this side of the river with the static."

I don't like it when adults second guess themselves. My stomach tightens and I get this weird metallic taste in my mouth. Shooptee squirms.

"We can do this," I say quietly, partly because they're making me nervous and partly because I really believe my pep talk. I expect everyone to take deep breaths, toss their heads back, and take off down the hall. No one moves. The Landions have to be looking for us by now. It's so quiet I can hear the Assassin Bug breathing on my shoulder.

The ball of fur in my arms wiggles. "Not last Shooptee left."

"Look," the Assassin Bug says, "I'm part of the reason we're all here. It seemed awful to stand by and watch an entire race of people disappear. What I did was completely against the rules, and I'd do it again. Everyone has been through a terrible ordeal, but we simply must keep going."

An arrow whizzes past my face. Handsome Lake ducks, falling into the wall.

"Run!" Shooptee yells.

My grandmother grabs me and Handsome Lake. "This way."

At the other end of the hall Landions march through a door. We take off running. Behind us, I hear their spears pounding on the stone floors. Run, turn, run, turn. I'm running so fast I don't even know who is close. I round the corner into a huge stone room. On the other side of the room, my messenger bag sits slumped on the floor. Our best chance of getting out of here alive is in that bag. I set Shooptee on the floor and run full speed across the enormous room. I slide like I've just hit a flyball and I'm stealing third base. Flipping the top flap open I see everything inside, except behind it, on the floor, they smashed the bottles of Honeysuckle juice. Fiery arrows will have to be good enough.

I turn around to grab Shooptee and run. Except he's not there. He's wandered off.

"*Shoop*," I whisper.

Across the room, Landions file through the doors with spears raised. At first only a few. Then so many I begin looking for an escape. There is no escape. I am literally in a corner. In a stone room with ceilings at least forty feet high.

I cannot be captured.

They'll lock us all away.

Maybe in the Killing Jars this time. No one knows we are here. No one will come looking for us.

Captured means we disappear forever.

Dozens of Landions run toward me. I have seconds to get out.

Seconds.

I do the only thing I can think of. I pull the sketchbook out. It's still wet and the pages stick together. I look up in time to see the first spear launched, headed straight for me. I squeeze my eyes shut. The hissing. The pounding. I fumble with the pages, flipping and ripping. Finally, I get to a blank page, wet, stuck to several others. My pen shoots straight up the page, to the right, then down.

I draw a door. Ink bleeds to the edges.

I don't have time to think about where.

Door or die.

Chapter Thirty-Six

I can't remember the last time I slept or ate or felt safe or did anything other than run and hold my breath. Everything has been falling apart for so long. I keep putting it back together, piece by piece, but it's not whole. Mine is a life held by little pieces of tape and glue and stubbornness.

I can hear the river, smell the damp stones. I lay my palm against a cold wall and open my eyes. Staying alive is a real priority. My eyes scan door after door as I look around.

"Montford," I whisper.

My stomach growls in reply. The tunnel looks empty. I don't know how to get back. This bouncing around through time isn't exactly a perfect science. I'm worried about Shooptee because he wandered off, though he seems to have been doing this a lot longer than me. This whole *Loops making leaps* thing is new to me.

I walk past door after door, hesitating in front of a few. I have no idea which door to choose.

Here I am.

In a tunnel.

Next to the River of Time.

Because that's totally normal.

I have no idea where I'm going.

I have no idea how to get back to where I've been.

I'm just really hoping that Handsome Lake and my Grandmother can get the clock piece and avoid capture.

Because, otherwise, *poof.*

I follow the River of Time past door after door, down long tunnels that twist and turn into new branches. Doors that lead to timelines I will never know. Doors of the past and doors of the future are so vast inside yet look exactly the same from the outside. Next to me, the present rushes onward. The Great Water Clock forever changed.

An endless river of endless time.

This whole experience feels huge. Like an essay question on the most important test of my life. I'm still not sure if I even have an answer. I am so tired. I am about to collapse when a few doors down I see a green scarab on a polished wood door. Metal cobras are carved on either side. No knobs or hinges. Just an enormous door in the shape of a keyhole, with a bright green beetle glinting in the lantern light. *The green beetle will take you home*, the Assassin Bug said.

My glitter green combat boots match the beetle perfectly. They feel heavy as I stumble forward, catching my balance, arriving upright in front of the huge, honey-colored door. I stare up at the green beetle as big as my head. Underneath, a message written in light reads:

Welcome Home

Laying my palms on the door, I stop and listen. We are forbidden to enter timelines that aren't our own. Rules are rules. I might not be so much for following the rules, but I've learned that walking through random doorways is dangerous. Closing my eyes, I gather my courage. This has to be the door. The only sound is of the river rushing behind me, water sloshing against stone.

This must be what the Assassin Bug was talking about. It has to be the way out. Maybe this door is some kind of short cut back to the farm.

"Montford," I whisper again.

Where's a mole when I need one?

I step back, look left then right. Not a single door comes close to this one.

I make a deal with myself.

If it opens, I go inside. No questions or taking forever to decide. Just go. I lay my hand on the metal and push. It glides open. It's dark inside the room so I feel around for a switch, hoping I don't get eaten by a giant snake.

Because I don't have a penny.

Or a jar of pickles.

Just a few fiery arrows and what's left of my courage.

I don't have a lot.

I have two tired hands.

Ten tired fingers.

Two tired feet.

One tired body.

And this blue-haired girl from Baltimore is ready to get back to the farm.

Chapter Thirty-Seven

Faint light slants across the windowpanes. My room in Baltimore is exactly how I left it. Not the day we moved, with tiny pieces of tape. The way it looked when I lived there. My bed, dresser, clothes on the floor. My favorite place on the planet was right here the whole time. A doorway I just had to cross through. A doorway I'd been walking past without knowing. A knob I was too afraid to turn. A message I didn't know how to read. A green beetle that shimmers in the lamplight. It was right here, all along.

There, standing at the wall, with a big black marker in his hand, is my father.

I suck in a stunned breath. "What are you doing here?"

Turning, he sees me across the room, and smiles. "I've been waiting here a long time."

I don't believe my eyes. This must be a trick, like Fong's Kitchen. A way to get me to relax so I can be dropped in a dark pit and eaten by giant insects.

"Don't worry." He extends a hand to me. "This part isn't a trick."

"How can you be here?"

"How can any of us be anywhere?"

Because here's the thing. I want him to be here. More than anything. I've never wanted something to be so real in all of my life. But I'm not sure this is how it works. "Are you saying you've been here all along? Are you saying you could have visited me?"

"Time is a little more complicated than that. You can move freely with your loops. I had to wait."

"You've been waiting here for six years?"

"Well, not waiting. More like expecting."

"What have you been doing?"

Gesturing to the walls, he says, "Drawing the story of how one blue-haired girl from Baltimore saves the world."

My eyes trail up the walls and I see, for the first time, that he's drawn cartoon panels from floor to ceiling with the black marker in his hand.

"Well, I'm doing a terrible job. I don't even know how to get back, and I had to leave everyone behind, and I'm scared."

When he says nothing my eyes trail back to the upper left corner. There I am on the burial mound. There I am with Rowan, out back, the first day I arrived at the farm. There I am with Shooptee in his cute little treehouse. There I am hiding in the branches from the Landions. Towering monsters with sharp teeth and black eyes who've come to destroy us all.

Chills run down my arms. "How did you know to draw this story?"

214

"It's a story as old as time itself. You just have to shut your mind off and listen. You have to lay back and dream. I was very good at dreaming back when we were all together."

"Until I dropped Wibbles and you fell down the stairs and died."

The corners of his mouth pinch down and it makes my stomach tighten. "I didn't die because I fell down the stairs, sweet girl. I fell down the stairs because I was dying."

"I don't understand."

"I didn't leave because of you or anything you asked me to do. I left because my time was up, there. Time is a diligent guardian."

"Well, you left us, and mom cried constantly. It was terrible. I suppose you couldn't hear it because you'd locked yourself away in this room. How could you do that? How could you come here and not tell me?"

He furrows his brow the way he always did when something upset him. "Do you know what it's like to be able to look back on every joy you ever had and not be able to have it anymore?"

I gesture around the room, too exhausted to keep my arms in the air for more than a few seconds. "Yes. I do."

Turning away from the wall completely, he caps the pen. He walks over to stand in front of me and takes my hand, pulling me in for a hug. His fingers are soft and warm and I squeeze them tight. This feels so real. *I want this to be real.*

"You and I have been through a lot," he whispers.

215

Tears push at the back of my eyes. "How long do I get to stay here with you?"

"Long enough for me to give you what you need for the next part of your journey."

I pull away. "I don't want that. I don't want to keep having everything taken away. This isn't fair. Who takes things away from little kids?"

He inhales sharply in the quiet room, and the sound feels like an arrow piercing my heart.

"You are such a brave blue-haired girl from Baltimore."

"I don't want to be brave. I just want us to all be together again. I want us all to go back to Baltimore and be happy."

"Except now you know that going back isn't the way to fix things."

I feel like my soul is sinking in a hole so small it disappears before I can blink back my tears.

"I don't care. I get a say in my own life. I choose to live here with you, in this room, forever."

He squeezes my hand. I don't want to squeeze back. I'm mad and confused. His fingers are long and sturdy, made to grasp pens and ideas floating through the air. Refusing to make eye contact, I stare down at my dirty jeans. I can see him out of the corner of my eye. He looks good. The way he did before he got sick and went away. Muscular arms pull me in for a bigger hug. I push back at first, but if this is real then I don't want to miss my one last chance. Still, my arms are at my sides. I just can't lift them on my own. I'm so tired and confused. I pull away and run to my bed. Diving in headfirst, it only takes me a second to feel the softness and know I am home. This bed. This room. This moment. It is everything to me, and yet I can't get myself to believe it.

Standing in the middle of the room, he asks, "Do you remember the story I used to tell you at bedtime? The one about how Maya Loop saves the world?"

My bottom lip pushes out and I hold it with my teeth. I will not cry. I will not fall apart in my favorite place in all the world. Not again. "Yes," I say quietly.

"Now you know stories aren't just stories. They are memories of other times. They play over and over again, in places that are very real, creating new doorways and branches."

I press my cheek into my soft pillow. "Why can't you come back with me? I mean, if you're here, why can't you exist anywhere?"

There is a long pause, much longer than I am comfortable with. Finally, he exhales. "Because this is the end of my timeline."

It is the saddest thing I've ever heard. I swing my legs around and sit upright. Scratches and dirt cover my arms. "I didn't come all of this way for goodbye." My face drops into my hands and I breathe. After all of this, how am I just supposed to accept the end? "After all that's happened, we're just supposed to give up and walk away?" My voice trembles and cracks. I look up at him for some clue that all of this isn't real. A clue that I'm in some dark pit making all of this up in my mind to stay alive.

"You're my favorite thing in all the world, back and forth, across time," he says softly. Nudging me gently, he points to the sketchpad. "That is my gift to you. The only important thing I could leave you with. Turn to a brand-new page and draw a door. Draw a door to the place you know you must return to."

"You're going to make me leave here, aren't you?"

"I can't make you leave this room. No one can. Only you decide if you want to save an entire race, and what that means to you."

I sigh. "In other words, draw a door to my greatest fear."

Leaning down to kiss my forehead, he says, barely above a whisper, "Forgiveness is the key. All you have to do is draw the door."

And just like that, it's all over.

A blip on a screen.

A dream I can barely remember.

An end that comes too soon after the beginning.

The place where two lines meet on a damp page and my precious old life disappears.

Chapter Thirty-Eight

A dusty hiss swirls through the air. My entire body freezes and I force myself to open my eyes. Thousands of Landions fill an enormous courtyard. In the center is the most magnificent clock I've ever seen. More magnificent than old, crumbling mansions back in Baltimore. A glimmering water clock in the shape of a mystic knot awaits one last piece. Built like a reverse waterfall, water rushes towards the top, loops under, around and back down where the river begins.

It would be the most beautiful sight in the world if everyone weren't held captive at the base.

Handsome Lake leans against the corner of the clock, blood dripping down his shoulder. My grandmother, Rowan, Spanky, Mr. Wibbles, and the Assassin Bug, along with hundreds of Shooptee, huddle under the tips of spears.

Metal scaffolding climbs as far as the eye can see, straight up the clock face.

My Shooptee spots me immediately and screams, "Help!"

A Landion's head snaps around in my direction. "Where is the piece, girl child?" The question is one long hiss. When I don't answer, he tosses his head back and roars so loud it makes the scaffold tremble.

An old anger swells in my gut. The kind I feel when kids push other kids around in the halls or take their lunch or steal their backpacks. The anger and fear that arises when I'm not sure I can make the situation right. The anger of helplessness. Bullies feed off of it. I try to swallow it back, but it stays. I don't know what to do. My sketchpad is in my hand, but it's not an option. Not now. Drawing a door will get me out of this mess but it leaves everyone else behind. Drawing a door doesn't prevent the Landions from finding that one final piece and erasing us all.

That is not an option.

The hissing starts up again. Another Landion roar. "Give us the clock piece or we kill you all, one by one."

"I'll never give you the clock piece," I squeeze my sketchbook and yell back.

"Very well," the Landion says, backing away.

Go girl power.

Obviously, my forceful tone scared him enough to back off. That's good, because except for a few fiery arrows I got nothing, including the clock piece. I flip my messenger bag open and stuff my sketchbook inside. I open my mouth to ask if I can take everyone home when I hear crying. Deep inside, my soul shivers like it's cracking loose.

At first, I can't see where the noise is coming from. Then the great crowd parts and a single Landion rolls Totsie in her wheelchair to the base of the clock.

Her puffy, red eyes land on me and she screams. A loud, awful scream, "Maya! Help me!! These monsters took me from my room."

Monsters. No longer just shadows in our world. Monsters with the power to steal us from our time. Real monsters. Evil monsters. The kind you can't just level up to avoid.

The kind who steal my friend to erase humans. There is no other word. *Monsters.* They have come for us all. Monsters who want total annihilation. The worst part is that I can't even stop to consider how awful all this is because it will make me cry, and crying is the very last thing I need. I haven't slept or eaten. I've spent this entire time just trying to keep everyone alive, including myself. I've been running from door to door trying to figure all this out and I still have no idea what to do.

Totsie grabs her wheels with both hands and pushes forward, but the Landion is too big, too strong. Tears stream down her cheeks as her tires spin. She pushes and pushes, trying to get her chair to roll forward.

The Landion holds the handle of her wheelchair and hisses, "The clock piece. I won't ask again."

I suspect the clock piece is at the bottom of the river. I just have to hold them off a little while longer.

"I don't have the clock piece," I yell.

"Shooptee have. Shooptee have," Shooptee screams.

Turning in that direction, I yell, "Never give them the clock piece."

A Landion snatches him up by his stubby little legs and holds him upside down.

"But I not the only Shooptee left," he yells. "I not the only Shooptee left. I save us."

I suck in a sharp breath as my eyes sweep over their sweet, furry faces. This is hard. Things change when people discover they aren't alone. Still, he cannot give up the clock piece.

"Don't give it to them!" I scream.

The Landion hoists Totsie's wheelchair high over his head, tilting it forward. She holds on tight, pushing back, but sliding. They are going to dump her on the floor like a real house of horrors.

"Maya," she screams, "*why are they doing this to me?*"

"Because they're mean," I scream.

Landions jab at her with tips of spears.

Rowan and Spanky and Mr. Wibbles put their fists up in the air.

The Landion shakes Shooptee, and he lets out a long howl.

I don't know if we can win this battle.

I don't know how long we can fight.

I don't know how long we can hold them off.

But I can't give up without trying.

A loud thud gets my attention. The clock piece is on the ground under Shooptee, rolling on its edge like a spinning top.

The Landion drops Shooptee and grabs the piece.

"*Noooooooooooo*!" I scream.

Shooptee trembles. "Shooptee hide in secret pouch." Shaking his head, he wails, "No. No. I sorry."

The Landion runs for the scaffold, climbing as fast as he can.

"NO! They cannot erase us."

Frantic, I pull one fiery arrow from my bag and hook it in my bow, because that's all I've got in my bag of tricks. With the arrow flaming, inches from my fingertips, I pull back hard on my string, hold it for only a second before launching it into the air. I whip the other arrow from my bag. I am about to let go of it when the first arrow strikes the clock piece and bursts into flames. The clock piece burns, crumbling at the feet of the Landion on the scaffold. Desperately, he tries to grab the pieces as they fall. A great gasp sweeps through the air. Sparks shoot from the clock piece and an enormous web appears.

All heads tilt back and look up into the sky. There, about halfway up the clock, dangling from a single, silken thread, is a spider with dazzling, diamond-shaped eyes.

"The Orb Weaver," my grandmother whispers.

The blind sparrow flies through the web, wobbly, and comes to rest on the ground. He looks so tiny in the roomful of giants.

"Reassembling the clock doesn't get rid of humans," he says.

A great hissing rises from the Landions. The shells of their bodies turn black, like their eyes, more evil and frightful than before.

"Silence," the blind sparrow says.

"Blind birds lie," a Landion says.

"The Landions tampered with time to rid themselves of humans after Handsome Lake locked them out. That is why they are here, on the other side of the river. But time does not like to be fooled. If the clock is not put back together in a mere four minutes, the Landions will cease to exist."

I'm confused. "But—that's not what they said."

"They are great deceivers."

"You have no authority here," a Landion booms, so loud the clock trembles.

"It's true," the Orb Weaver says, "What the sparrow says is true."

"Lies," the Landions chant.

"Silence," the Orb Weaver yells.

The Assassin Bug climbs to my grandmother's shoulder. After clearing his throat, he asks, "Do you want to keep deceiving, or do you want to survive?"

The Landions fall quiet.

The rich, black color of their bodies fades back to tan. They stand very still.

"You, of all people, know the power the Loops have," the blind sparrow says.

"Plead your case," the Orb Weaver instructs.

"But—" a Landion starts.

"Three minutes, forty seconds," the Assassin Bug says. "Time waits for no one."

"You have no power here," the Landion yells to the Orb Weaver.

"I do when I am summoned," she says.

"No one summoned you, arachnid."

The tiny sound of someone clearing his throat emanates from the center of the army of Landions.

"I did."

I know the voice immediately.

A minute later, Montford emerges from the towering bugs, waddling across the floor with his big hands held high and his nose twitching.

Landions hiss, making a *skeet skeet* noise, a field of doom.

"Leave the mole be. He speaks the truth."

"Liars in the holes."

"Stop it," the Orb Weaver yells. "Stop it. This is how you ended up here. I will not let you tarnish the good name of the moles who have faithfully served since the beginning."

"Yeah," Montford says, wagging a round finger at the giants glaring down at him on the stone floor. "I know what you're up to. Moles have excellent hearing, you know. I heard your scheming."

"Silence!"

"You have no power over us," the Orb Weaver says.

"We have the power to destroy," the Landions yell.

"Your power to destroy is destroying you."

The tips of spears, pointed at everyone in the center, begin to tremble.

"Tell the girl child and save yourselves."

The Landions hiss and pound their spears. *Boom, boom, boom.* Between each *boom*, a seething *hiss* holds all the *boom*s together. Totsie holds tight, tears streaming down her cheeks. I reach out my hand, but she is so far away.

Montford smooths his fur, looking up at the giants. "Putting the clock piece back doesn't erase humans. If the clock isn't reconstructed, the Landions are erased."

"And you only have two minutes," the Orb Weaver says.

I look up at their black, shiny eyes and gnashing, sharp teeth.

"You're monsters and you're liars and you put my friends in jars," I scream, feeling the hot tears burn my cheeks.

"Why couldn't you just ask for help?" my grandmother asks quietly.

The hissing stops and they turn, pointing their sharp bug fingers. "Because who would help us? No one, that's who. Look at how everyone came to help the humans. It's always the same. It doesn't matter how awful you are, someone always comes to help you. Saving you means saving us."

The Landions snarl and hiss.

I don't budge. I've got one fiery arrow, and I'm not afraid to use it.

Standoff.

Old school, playground style.

No budge.

First one to blink, loses.

Put up or shut up.

I can hear Rowan, Handsome Lake, and my grandmother breathing, sharp spears against their cheeks.

"Two and a half minutes," the Orb Weaver says.

The Landion opens his enormous mouth full of sharp teeth and hisses so loud, he blows the hair off my forehead. His breath is hot, and smells like car exhaust. I don't move. I don't blink. I open my mouth wide and, from the deepest part of my gut, I hiss back.

They fall silent. The Landion slowly sets Totsie's wheelchair on the ground. With lightning speed, she rolls immediately to my side, grabbing the edge of my hoodie.

"You are monsters," I scream. "All of you."

Totsie squeezes my hand tight.

I don't know how to get us back to Baltimore. Maybe I can draw a door. Maybe I can get us back to the door with the green beetle and use it as a short cut. All I know is that we need to leave. I lower my bow and hold it with one hand. I must save us and figure out a way to destroy the door to their world. I back up, holding tight to Totsie's hand. We make it to the center where my grandmother grabs my other hand.

"We have to help them, " she whispers.

"What? No. How can you say that? *They put you in a jar.*"

The clock groans. Full of mystery and wonder, it's fractured with a piece missing, just like me. I have no idea what will happen if I am whole. This clock is like the pieces of my soul I need to light the dark challenge ahead. Staring up at the curves of the knot with the charred place where I shot the arrow I know. I know me and this clock are linked somehow. The same way I knew about the Landions. I drew their dark eyes and stuck them to the refrigerator back home. Home is so far away now. So far that I have absolutely no idea how to get back.

I suddenly feel like I am the clock, and if I can just squeeze that one last piece into place, I will be whole.

I shiver, remembering my father say, "Forgiveness is the key."

All the tears I've swallowed back come now.

Hot and burning down my cheeks.

"I will not forgive you for what you've done," I scream.

Every single Landion turns to look at me. Their black eyes fill with tears and turn the color of warm sunsets.

"Nothing!" I scream. "I will never forgive you."

This is a trick.

A trick to make me feel sorry for monsters.

Which I don't.

I want them all to disappear.

I look up at the clock and yell, "Take them all away forever. I hate them."

A Landion pinches up his face. "Hate is a terrible thing to hold onto."

I sweep my arm in front of my body, like I'm leveling a field. "You're all going to be destroyed."

The Orb Weaver watches me from her dangling silken thread. "Is that your final word?"

My eyes shoot up to her dazzling eyes. "Why would I choose anything else?"

"Because maybe they have something to offer you in return."

"What could they possibly offer me?"

The Landions turn and look out to the side. One nudges another, who nudges another, all the way to the back of the line where the desert rolls away. A second later, I see they are passing something to the front. The edges of their bodies begin to fade.

Without saying a word, a single Landion steps from the crowd and sets a bag of mini powdered doughnuts on the ground at my feet.

I look down at the bag and shake my head. This battle is not won with a bag of doughnuts.

Still fading, the Landions turn to walk away, heads down, tears flowing over the sand to the river.

I don't know what to do.

"Wait," I choke back tears. "Wait."

They stop and turn.

"Have *you* ever had a mini powdered doughnut?" I ask.

A Landion shakes his head.

I push the bag with my glitter green combat boot. "Try one."

"I—" he starts.

"You can't say you've lived until you have a mini powdered doughnut. It's the law, back in Baltimore."

Fading too quickly to open the bag, I grab it. With one quick rip, a puff of powdered sugar floats into the air. Sweet, sugared, vanilla doughnut bliss. I want to eat the whole bag, but this might be the most important time to share.

I inhale deeply. "Go on," I say.

I put one doughnut in his mouth. He squeezes his eyes shut like it's going to hurt.

A second later, his eyes pop open. Smiling and chewing, he says, "Oh, my! How do you eat just one?"

"You don't," I shrug. "You eat the whole bag."

Landions have a soft covering of fur on their face, and when they aren't trying to eat me alive, they're not nearly as scary.

Out of the corner of my eye, I see Rowan watching me. Everyone is waiting.

"Well, that's just about the best thing in the world," the Landion says.

I totally agree. I allow myself one mini powdered doughnut. As the sweetness covers my tongue, I suddenly have an idea. I grab my sketchbook and run for the one empty space on the enormous clock. Without stopping to explain, I climb the scaffolding in a flash. My glitter green combat boots slam against the metal. I climb and climb until I reach the place where the one piece is missing.

I flip to an empty page. I squeeze my eyes shut, remembering the clock piece I grabbed from the kitchen. I scribble and color in the lines. I swoop and scratch and draw. I recreate all the details on the page, then rip it out of my book. It's the only page I've ever ripped

230

from my book, and little sparks fly. Shoving my sketchpad into my bag, I feel around. I whip out my roll of tape. Not even sure if it will work, I hold the piece of paper and tape it in place.

This has to work.

It has to be the right thing to do.

I run my fingers over the last few pieces of tape to smooth out the edges.

The great clock groans.

Surprised, I step back.

My heart speeds up.

I call up to the Orb Weaver as the gears begin to turn. "What if I really put the clock back together?"

"I will weave everyone into a new timeline, but I can't guarantee I can do it fast enough, or for everyone. I can't promise we all survive."

That doesn't sound promising. I run back down the scaffolding and grab the bag of doughnuts. Water splashes from the clock. The ground begins to shake. I drop one more mini powdered doughnut on my tongue.

It tastes like home.

Totsie squeezes the armrest of her chair. "I believe in you, Maya Loop," she whispers.

I close my eyes.

"What if we never make it home?" Rowan's voice quivers.

I swallow back my own fear and open my eyes. The last clock piece clicks into place. The sound of metal grinding and water rushing is deafening. A blitz of water is pushed into the knot. Just when I think we're all about to be swallowed in a flood, the Orb Weaver whips me up into the web. I suck in a breath as I feel the silken threads spin fast around my body. I am just about to ask what will happen when everything goes black and I feel that familiar *whomp*.

in the end …

I land in the middle of the gravel driveway. In front of me, the big farmhouse rises from the earth like a magnificent sign. A sign I made it back. The words echo in my head. *I made it back.* The setting sun glistens over tips of winter wheat. The smell of dirt and grass and barn fills my lungs. I dust myself off, though it hardly matters. Looking down at my clothes I realize I'm dirty from head to toe. Off in the distance, a horse snorts. It's like the greatest sound in the world.

The sound of victory.

The screen door of the farmhouse creaks open and Granddaddy walks onto the old boards of the porch. Everything here is old, a reminder we Loops have been leaping a long time. A reminder we can keep going as long as these sturdy boards stick together. A reminder that we've been carving a place for ourselves in time. He squints, realizes it's me, and his whole face bursts into this crazy smile.

He yells, "Honey, she's here. She's here just like you said."

Running down the steps two at a time, he waves, and I realize he's holding a jar of homemade pickles in one hand. It's such a bizarre, ridiculous thing, but I've never been so happy to see a jar of pickles in all my life.

I wish Shooptee was here.

Behind Granddaddy, the screen door opens and my grandmother walks out onto the porch. The last rays of light roll over her shoulders and she looks strong and beautiful, arms out to her sides. She takes a deep breath, one that fills her lungs, and she holds it, finally free of the killing jar. It's then I get my glitter green combat boots to move, and I run. Run with energy I didn't even know I had, towards a finish line I never imagined.

Behind my grandmother, Rowan and his dad step out of the farmhouse.

She made it.

He made it.

We made it.

I made it.

I did this, I think to myself.

I did this, I repeat over and over in my head.

Up on the roof, the Assassin Bug stands next to Montford, waving.

I can see them perfectly.

This is real, I think to myself.

Montford smiles so big his whiskers twitch.

Here we are.

I thought we would lose it all, but we pulled off the greatest level up I've ever witnessed in my life.

Tears push against my eyelids. Tears I usually try to hide. Those weird, happy tears that come when everything feels overwhelming but good. Granddaddy stumbles in the gravel, but he's running so fast he barely notices. His long legs cover the distance, and within seconds he swoops me into the air, whooping, spinning me around in a circle.

The world spins and spins. I hear cheering from the porch. Mr. Wibbles falls out of my messenger bag and lands in the dust. He's a stuffed animal again, but I know in some other time he's real. I can't explain it, but I know it deep in my heart.

I can't explain how I made it through that journey.

I can't explain rivers of time and moles with aviator goggles and Assassin Bugs and Shooptees that live in trees and Landions who'll stop at nothing to stay alive.

But I do know one thing.

Blue-haired girls from Baltimore never give up.

About the Author

If you loved this novel then follow

Lis Anna-Langston

on GOODREADS & AMAZON

for new releases, updates, and giveaways or subscribe at

www.lisannalangston.com.

LIS ANNA-LANGSTON was raised along the winding current of the Mississippi River on a steady diet of dog-eared books. She attended a Creative and Performing Arts School from middle school until graduation and went on to study Literature at Webster University. Her two novels, Gobbledy and Tupelo Honey have won the Parents' Choice Gold, Moonbeam Book Award, Independent Press Award and NYC Big Book Awards. Twice nominated for the Pushcart award, a Finalist in the Brighthorse Book Prize, William Faulkner Fiction Award & Thomas Wolfe Fiction Award, her work has been published in The Literary Review, The Merrimack Review, Emrys Journal, The MacGuffin, Sand Hill Review and dozens of other literary journals.

She draws badly, sings loudly, loves ketchup, starry skies & stories with happy aliens.

You can find her in the wilds of South Carolina plucking stories out of thin air.

Praise for other titles

Gobbledy

"Hugely entertaining as well as emotionally moving."

—*Kirkus Reviews*

"A delightfully entertaining novel by an author with a genuine flair for originality and the kind of narrative storytelling style that will fully engage the imaginative attention of appreciative young readers ages 8-11, *Gobbledy* by Lis Anna-Langston . . . will prove to be an immediate and enduringly popular addition to elementary school, middle school, and community library collections."

—*Midwest Book Review*

"*The Wonder Years* meets *A Christmas Story* meets *E.T.* in this magical novel with dialogue that snaps, crackles, and pops, and a narrative that skips, jumps, and hops from one delightful surprise after the other. Yet beneath the magic and fun there is an undercurrent of sorrow and loss each character is trying to move through, for this will be the first Kissmas without Dexter and D-man's beloved mother. How these characters—and their furry little alien sidekick—navigate this strange and complicated time in their lives will amaze and inspire you. Young adults and old adults alike will love the adventures that await inside these pages."

—Cathy Smith Bowers, former Poet Laureate of North Carolina, and South Carolina Authors' Hall of Fame Inductee

Tupelo Honey

A loveable, engaging, original voice, Tupelo brightens this accomplished tale of dysfunction in a family where "nothing had ever been right.".

~ Publishers Weekly ~

From the delicious title (the spunky 11-year-old narrator was named after Elvis' birthplace) to every last unconventional character and careful detail, Tupelo Honey is a delight. Set in rural Mississippi, with a cast of colorful southerners, it stars one pretty dysfunctional family at the center of which is Tupelo Honey. Author Lis Anna-Langston gets into the head of her title girl completely, taking readers on a ride of a sort of haunted but beautiful mess.

It's certainly not a dull life, one full of heartbreaks big and small, but this tough sweet girl pulls it off with aplomb. It's a treat from start to end. Langston has written rich, vivid characters, and painted a vibrant mosaic of a year in one young southern girl's life. It's a hard book to put down, and one you won't want to end. I envy its future readers.

~ Teresa DiFalco ©2016 Parents' Choice ~

When you read more than a hundred books per year, it's exciting to find one that surprises you. "Tupelo Honey" by Lis Anna Langston is one of those, sneaking up quietly to bust expectations and leaves you thinking about the story long after closing the book.

~ Chanticleer Book Reviews ~

Acknowledgements

This novel began as a conversation with my daughter and culminated as a NaNoWriMo project that I dove into with incredible passion.

I'd first like to thank my daughter for her amazing view of the world.

To my husband I am eternally grateful for his love and massive support. He typed every draft of this novel and gave me incredible advice.

J. Thomas Meador read every draft of this novel and workshopped with me across time and borders as we both moved around this country.

Coming Soon!

Look for my new title

Flickers

CPSIA information can be obtained
at www.ICGtesting.com
Printed in the USA
LVHW030902090721
692197LV00003B/290